Other  titles

Magenta in the Pink

ECHO FREER

Hodder
Children's
Books

a division of Hachette Children's Books

Acknowledgements: I'd like to thank my son Jacob for his technical know-how, Imogen Wiltshire, Verien Wiltshire, Michael Kelly and Seema Gulati for all their contributions and advice, and my late brother, Martin Freer Sunley for inspiring some of Magenta's antics.

First published in Great Britain in 2002
by Hodder Children's Books

This edition published in 2007

A Catalogue record for this book is available from the British Library

ISBN-13: 978 0 340 95074 6

Typeset by Avon Dataset Ltd, Bidford-on-Avon, Warks

Printed and bound in Great Britain by Clays Ltd, St Ives plc

The paper and board used in this paperback by Hodder Children's Books are natural recyclable products made from wood grown in sustainable forests. The manufacturing processes conform to the environmental regulations of the country of origin.

Hodder Children's Books
a division of Hachette Children's Books
338 Euston Road
London NW1 3BH

For Mo, Vee and Yak – with all my love.

1
Magenta

Parents can be so unreasonable sometimes! Take my dad. I mean, I thought my request was perfectly understandable in the circumstances.

'I want to move!'

I'd been back at school two weeks and things were definitely not going according to plan.

'You haven't finished your dinner yet.'

Dinner – now there's a word to be taken in its loosest possible sense. Gran does most of the cooking in our house – unless Dad decides to do his Ainsley Harriot impersonation or I've had the misfortune to have done Food Technology that day. Unfortunately Gran's more adept with a set of spanners than she is with an egg whisk. She's from the *Cordon Noir* school of cookery: if it doesn't come out of a pre-packed carton with the instructions written in 'Dinners for Dummies' language, it's pretty hard to distinguish the food on the plate from your average lump of smokeless fuel. Today's attempt *had* been cauliflower cheese (note the past tense).

So there I was, in a state of extreme anxiety about

my life in general and having the additional worry of desperately trying to think how to dispose of the stuff on my plate. Trust me, I'm not exaggerating when I say it looked more like a miniature prehistoric forest recently unearthed by archaeologists, than anything that could even remotely be construed as having nutritional value. It was all brown and slimy and the thought of putting any of it into my mouth was about as appealing as lying naked in a bath full of slugs. I could tell from Dad's voice that he was desperate for some moral support at the table but he'd completely missed my point.

'No, I don't mean move from the table,' (although that probably wasn't a bad idea as there was plum crumble and something vaguely resembling yellow concrete for pudding) 'I mean *move*. Move house.'

'What!' Talk about irony. The first time in weeks that Dad and Gran had actually agreed on anything, and they chose now to unite against me. I suppose I should have been relieved that they were communicating at all after the motorbike incident (Gran had been caught bombing around the neighbourhood with Auntie Venice, terrorising innocent road users) but, I have to say, I thought their combined decibel level was a bit of an over-reaction.

'I just think it's time we moved on,' I said, pushing the carboniferous goo round my plate and trying to sound nonchalant. 'You know, rolling stones gather no moss and all that.'

Dad and Gran were both staring at me very suspiciously. 'Are you in trouble at school again?'

Honestly! Thanks for the vote of confidence, Dad. But I didn't say that. I played it really cool and called Sirius over. (Sirius is my dog. He's named after Sirius the Dog Star because my dad's an amateur astronomer – *very* amateur, actually.) Anyway, I called Sirius partly as a distraction and partly in the hope that I would be able to slip him some cauliflower cheese without Gran seeing.

'Of course not!' I was genuinely offended because, actually, it was true. I was quite proud of myself having gone two whole weeks without incident – well, not counting my exam results but they're not really an *incident* – they're more the unavoidable result of my unfortunate injury at the Christmas party. Which, when you think about it, was the school's fault anyway. 'But, you know, we've lived here for what – ten years now, Dad?' Dad and I moved in with Gran when I was three, just after my mum died. 'Ten years is a long time in anyone's books. I mean, it's a whole decade stuck in one place.

And what about you, Gran? Surely you must be ready for a change after, what is it—'

'Forty-one years and eight months.' (Ooops! I hadn't realised it was *quite* that long.) 'I moved here as a new bride, your father and Uncle Wayne were both born in this house and your granddad was buried from here, so whatever's going on, Magenta, you can think again about moving. Any more cauliflower cheese for anyone?'

Dad put on this yucky grin. 'Er, no thanks, Mum, but that was delicious.' Why is it OK for adults to lie but not for kids?

Then he turned his attention back to me. 'So, come on, Magenta. We're not stupid, you know.' Now, I don't know about you, but I always think that sort of statement is worthy of debate, but Dad was sitting with his eyebrows raised and Gran was holding the plum crumble in a distinctly menacing manner, so I decided to let it go. 'Is this to do with Daniel?'

'No!' I said, flicking the last piece of incinerated cauliflower in Sirius' direction, while Gran had her back turned trying to lever the custard into a jug. I pushed my chair back and made as though I was going to storm out. I thought a teenage tantrum would be a more tactful way of getting out of the pudding situation than a straightforward refusal.

Unfortunately my foot slipped in something squelchy and I did the splits rather inelegantly on the kitchen floor. (It seemed that not even Sirius could bring himself to eat Gran's offering.) I reached out to steady myself but the only thing to come to hand was the corner of the tablecloth and – well, I'm sure you can imagine the rest. Not a pretty sight! There was broken crockery everywhere and little wizened brown lumps flying across the kitchen like cannonballs. (It turned out that, in their heyday, they'd been plums!)

'Now, young lady, let that be a lesson to you.' Honestly, don't you just hate it when parents say that? 'I won't tolerate temper tantrums, so you can go and get a dustpan and brush and clear this lot up before Belinda comes round.'

So there I was, sitting on the floor, surrounded by the remnants of Gran's scorched earth policy and I thought, could my life be any worse? I mean, let's examine the facts:

a) my dad's girlfriend, Belinda, only happens to be my Art teacher – which means that
b) I am having serious doubts about taking Art as one of my GCSE options – because
c) everyone will think that if I get a good mark (which I probably would've done) that either

she'd been biased when she marked it or she'd given me significant amounts of help – so

d) I'm having to re-think my options and none of the teachers seems to want me in their group (don't even go there!) – which means that

e) I've got lumbered with Geography which I hate *and* (most hurtful of all),

f) Daniel next-door, who was a really good friend to me for ten years, conned me into going out with him and then double-crossed me with a girl who's old enough to be his . . . well, his older sister, anyway. I saw them with my own eyes! Add to that the fact that,

g) I spent the Christmas holidays with my hands bandaged up like *Return of the Mummy* because at the school Christmas party the toilets collapsed and my fingers got trapped and you'll see why my 'new-start-in-a-new-area' idea was such a stroke of genius.

I *had* thought that life was running smoothly for a change. I mean, apart from the fact that I was severely incapacitated in the finger region, the rest of the Christmas holidays had been great. For the first time in the living memory of your average elephant, we'd stayed at home for Christmas and hadn't gone to spend it with my aunt and uncle and the cousins from hell. I'd even begun to think that Daniel really was quite fanciable and, being the mature and forgiving person that I am, I have to admit that the double-crossing, two-timing scumbag is the most fantastic kisser ever! Although, with hindsight, that's probably because he's had so much practice. Anyway, that's all ancient history now.

Of course, one of the worst things about the Christmas holidays is that we were expected to revise, because we went back to school and straight into our practice SATs. I mean, who in their right mind is going to spend their Christmas holidays revising? Only a total boffin! I'll admit that quite a few times when I was still going out with Daniel, the snake, we did sit in his room with our books out. But, to be honest, my Michelin-man finger-wear made it a teensy bit difficult to turn the pages. And holding a pen to make notes was practically impossible. So I let Daniel do the revision for both of us. And teachers always do say it's good to revise in pairs.

'I'll test you,' Daniel said one evening. He was lying on his back, holding his book away from me and pretending to show me the page then flicking it away again and laughing. 'OK, name the three ways heat is transferred.'

I was lying on my tummy and thinking how dreamy he looked with his new hairstyle. 'Erm, boiling the kettle, turning on the cooker and lighting the fire,' I replied, wondering how I'd managed not to notice how lovely he was for all those years. (Little did I know, at that stage, what a slimeball he really was.)

He started to smile at me (Oooo, it was such a lovely smile. I remember, I went all gooey) and then he put his arms round me and gave me this absolutely fabulous kiss. (Looking back, I can't believe I was so deluded!) 'You're so funny, you know, Magenta.' Funny? It wasn't quite the compliment I'd been looking for, but his voice sounded affectionate, so I went along with it. Then he gave me this strange look. 'You do know that the answer's radiation, convection and conduction, right?'

'Course I do!' I tried to look hurt and made a mental note to write it down as soon as I could hold a pen. Maybe my tutor group hadn't covered that yet. Daniel's lot always seem to be streets ahead of us on everything.

So you see, it's not fair to say that I didn't do *any* revision. Not that some teachers believed that. I was going to drop History at the end of this year anyway. The teacher, Jones the Bones, just loved humiliating me. The last lesson we'd had he'd found particularly amusing.

'So Miss Orange, please enlighten us again as to the name of the Italian leader during World War II.' Personally, I think he's been teaching about dictators for so long, he's actually become one. I mean how was I supposed to know, for heavens' sake? But I was getting the distinct impression that my answer of 'The Pope' was way off the mark.

Science wasn't much better. Mr Smedley, or Smelly, had asked me to see him in the staffroom at lunchtime to talk about my Science paper. I was on my way over thinking that, even though my academic career seemed to have hit a bit of a block, at least my love life was thriving when, just as I passed the sixth-form block, the door opened and I saw Daniel coming out. He was talking to this girl who, and I say this without a hint of jealousy, would've given Britney Spears a good run for her money. And she was flirting with him outrageously. I know it sounds far-fetched because she's Year 12 and Daniel's only Year 9 but, let's face it, at the Christmas party he had half Year 10 fancying him, so it's not beyond the realms of possibility. I hid behind one of the columns in the entrance lobby and watched the two of them. She had her hand on the doorframe and was leaning towards him in this really flirtatious way. I mean, she was *so* coming on to him. And he was smiling at her and laughing in this really false way. I could hardly believe my eyes.

Just then I saw Smelly shuffling along the corridor towards the staffroom. I didn't want either Smelly *or* Daniel to see me, so I hid behind the column until the coast was clear. I couldn't hear what Daniel was saying but then I heard the Year 12 girl say, 'So see you tonight then. My place at about half-seven – OK?' What a cradle-snatcher!

I poked my head round the pillar and saw Daniel as he walked away. He did this ridiculous hop-step-and-a-jump and punched the air like he'd just scored the winning goal. I was gutted! All that rubbish he's been saying about liking me for years and never having felt like this about anyone else. What a mongrel! And, worse still, what a fool I'd been to believe him!

I decided at that moment that Smelly and his Science paper could wait: there were more important issues to be settled. I was just heading off after Daniel when a voice like a circular saw echoed round the lobby.

'Ah, Miss Orange! What a fortunate coincidence!'

Mrs Delaney, my head of year (more commonly referred to as Mrs Blobby because of her uncanny resemblance to a whale with acne and her disgusting love of all varieties of pink clothing), was bearing down on me. Oh, deep joy! What else was life going to throw at me today? 'Just the person I've been talking about.' I got the distinct impression that she didn't mean that in a good way. 'There has been some concern amongst the staff about your practice SAT results, Magenta.' She was leading me off along the corridor towards her office which was in completely the opposite direction from the way Daniel had gone. And, call me psychic, but I just knew it wouldn't be in my interest to tell her that this wasn't a good time to talk. 'In your Key Stage 2 SATs you averaged level five to six, am I correct?' The door of her office shut behind us with this horrible death-knell sound.

'Yes, Mrs Delaney.' It was true; I'd been one of the cleverest at primary school.

'In fact, you were considered one of our brighter pupils, were you not?'

I gave a modest shrug. I mean, one doesn't like to brag, does one?

'So I'm wondering whether these, let's say, *disappointing*, results are a reflection of the general deterioration in your attitude which began last term, or whether they are a result of the unfortunate injury you sustained before Christmas.'

'Oh, it's because of my hands. Definitely!'

'Well, we shall see.' There was something weird about the way she said it. I mean, let's face it, I have never been Mrs Blobby's favourite pupil. 'I've seen the Head this morning, Magenta, and he has taken the unprecedented move of offering you a second chance.' I think I was expected to grovel with gratitude at this point but I was feeling a teensy bit suspicious. 'You will be considered to have been absent through injury last week. So, beginning next Monday, you will re-sit your exams.'

'What?' How could this horror be happening to me? As if *one* lot of tests wasn't bad enough!

'You will report to this office with your pens and pencils and, now that your fingers seem fully recovered, this time you will be able to do yourself justice.'

I was just thinking that maybe it wasn't so bad – I mean, all I had to do was get copies of Seema's papers and learn her answers off by heart – when the Blob went in for the kill.

'Of course, the staff will be providing me with past papers so that the exam is fair. It would hardly do for you to be asked the same questions now that you've had an opportunity to see the papers and go over them, would it?' *Gggrrr!* What was she, a mind-reader or something?

But even that wasn't the worst thing to happen. I didn't manage to find Daniel before the bell went, so I had to endure an entire afternoon of Technology with the image of him and his sixth-form slapper in my head. And even worse, this term my group's doing Resistant Materials in DT and we're supposed to be designing a toy suitable for a primary school child. Honestly, the only primary school child I know is my cousin Holden and I'd need access to either explosive material or lethal insects to design a toy for him – they're about the only things that hold any interest for him. I don't know where Uncle Wayne and Auntie Heather have gone wrong. I mean, my dad's been on his own (well – ish, apart from Gran, that is) and yet he's managed to bring me up to be normal, balanced and fun to be with. But Holden and his sister, Justine, have had two parents bringing them up and they're such total social embarrassments I can't believe we're related.

So, anyway, I spent the afternoon trying to design this stupid toy for my stupid brat of a cousin and trying not to think of Daniel and his stupid flirty sixth-former or the fact that I was going to have to sit my stupid exams again. The lesson seemed to go on for about a hundred years. By the end of it I just wanted to get out of school and go home. I was just on my way across the car park when Daniel called out after me.

'Hang on, Magenta!' He'd obviously been running. 'Where're you going?'

'Home!' I carried on walking and couldn't bring myself to look at the louse.

'Weren't you going to wait for me?' He tried to hold my hand but I snatched it away. I wasn't going to fall for his slimy charm like that brainless Year 12 girl.

'Magenta, are you mad at me or something?'

The nerve of the toad! 'Why? Is there some reason why I should be mad at you?'

'No, but you seem upset.' He was practically running to keep up with me.

Upset? I'll give him upset! I stopped walking and looked him straight in the eye. 'Well, maybe you'd like to explain about lunchtime?'

'Lunchtime?' I knew he was just stalling; trying to give himself time to think up some excuse. 'Is this because I didn't meet you for lunch? Look, I'm sorry Magenta, but I had to see someone.' Talk about a smooth talker!

I remembered what Gran had said once; if you give

14

a person enough rope, they'll hang themselves. I decided to play it cool. 'It must've been someone really important. Was it a teacher?'

'No,' he said, looking a bit sheepish. 'Look, it's all a big secret but if you promise not to say anything . . .' I nodded my head. 'I had to meet Sam . . .' Then he went the same colour as Mrs Blobby's cardigan and started kicking the ground. I looked up and there she was: the sixth former he'd been talking to at lunchtime.

'Hi, Dan,' she said, as she walked past. Dan! *Dan?*

'Er, hi!' he said, looking guiltier than a compulsive liar on a lie detector.

So he was calling himself Dan now, was he? Daniel was OK for me but it was too babyish for Year 12 girls, was it? And trying to tell me he'd been meeting Sam! As if I'd be that gullible. I'd seen and heard enough.

'Fine!' I said. 'I'm going home, Daniel – on my own!'

'Wait! Magenta! You don't understand.'

'No, I don't.' On that score he was one hundred per cent right. I didn't understand how one minute he could be telling me how much I meant to him and the next he was lying and cheating on me. 'But why don't you try and explain it to me tonight?' I'd heard him agreeing to go and see that cradle-snatcher, so I knew this would be crunch time. 'Let's see – how about if I come round to yours at about – say, half-seven? How's that?'

'Erm – I can't make it tonight. I'm sorry.' He was squirming. 'But look, how about I take you out on Saturday? We could go bowling, or to the cinema, or . . .'

'Forget it, Daniel – or do you prefer to be called *Dan* these days?' And I started to walk off. I was so mad. The least I expected from my first relationship was honesty and he'd done nothing but lie to me. I was fuming! I turned round and shouted at him. 'It's over, Daniel! We're finished.' And I left him standing by the school gate. Honestly, the way he was opening and closing his mouth it was like feeding time at the aquarium.

So that's when I thought, it's time to move on. New beginnings and all that. We could go to Manchester so that Dad could be nearer to his brother . . . or Cornwall – think of all the surfers in summer. Oh yes! Cornwall would be *brilliant!*

2
Daniel

I do not understand girls at all! One minute Magenta's all over me, saying things like, 'Ooo, I'm so glad we got together, Daniel,' and, 'Ooo, you're so lovely, Daniel,' and, 'Ooo, I can't believe we've lived next door to each other for so long and haven't thought of going out before now.' And the next she's throwing a complete wobbler just because I didn't spend one measly lunchtime with her. Over-reaction or what?

I tried talking to my mum about it – she's usually quite good with problems and stuff like that but all she could come up with was, 'The path of true love ne'er did run smooth.' I mean, what use is that? And, to be honest, if *this* is true love, then I don't want to know. In fact, I'm going to give up on girls for good. I mean, last year I tried to do the decent thing and finish with Arlette in a kind and sensitive way, but what did I get? Two weeks of grief with her blubbing down the phone every night while practically every other girl in our year froze me out. Going to school was like being on a field trip to

Siberia. Talk about women being from Venus!

Then, just when I was thinking that life had finally answered all my dreams and brought Magenta to me, the love of my life, it all goes pear-shaped again. We had four fantastic, but I have to say very short, weeks together . . . Anyway, I don't even want to go there any more because just when things were looking sweet, she goes totally ape and dumps me – all because I don't spend one stupid lunchbreak with her. And it's not like I didn't try.

The thing is, right, ever since I was one of the supporting DJs at the youth club rave last October, I've been experimenting on my brother Joe's turntables. He's so wrapped up in his girlfriend, Anthea Pritchard, that he's hardly used them for ages, so I've been nipping into his room and having a little mix on the old demon decks whenever he's out. And I know I shouldn't brag, but I've actually got quite good. Then, before Christmas, I was talking to Mr Behl, our teacher, about my options and he reckoned I'd be great to take Systems and Control for Technology. And I got to thinking that that *would* be wicked – I could design flashing lights to go with the music and everything. I could set up my own mobile disco and earn loads of cash, which would be so much better than the car-washing business.

Anyway, I got really excited about it all. It seemed as though my life was finally getting sorted. Magenta and I were officially regarded as an item and it was really cool.

For the first time her family stayed at home for Christmas, so we spent every day together. I mean, boom or what! I made sure I'd got mistletoe everywhere in my bedroom – which, actually caused a bit of trauma when Sirius came round with her one day, because he ate some of the berries that had fallen off and was sick all over my duvet. It was a bit of a passion-killer but, after that, we were much more careful and it was just snogsville the whole time. Except when we did our revision together, of course – we had to stop then. But, she was so cute the way she teased me with her funny little answers. She's so great. I felt really sorry for her though, because she was in such a lot of pain after the accident with the collapsing toilets and she still couldn't write properly when it came to doing our practice SATs, so her results weren't that good. Poor Magenta! She was really worried about what her dad was going to say . . . Come to think of it, I wonder if *that's* why she was so upset that I hadn't been with her at lunchtime? I mean, if she'd had some more results and needed my support, I really should've been there for her. No *wonder* she was mad at me! Although, as Spud said, she didn't even give me a chance to explain.

You see, I was changing lessons this morning when this girl in the sixth form grabbed my arm. 'Are you Daniel Davis?'

I must admit, she was pretty cool and Spud could hardly believe his eyes. Spud's my mate, Sam Pudmore, who fancies the socks off Magenta and, through a gross error of judgement on her part, actually got more than a kiss off her at the youth club disco – but we won't go into that.

'Ye-errh,' I sort of spluttered.

'Hi, I'm Samantha Campion. Can we have a chat?' She beckoned me over into the doorway of the caretaker's room.

'Errm . . .' I followed, but was totally confused. 'Have I done something wrong?' I thought perhaps The Crusher (Mr Crusham, the Head) had suddenly appointed all Year 12s as Archimedes High's military junta and I'd been inadvertently walking on the wrong side of the corridor or my tie was the wrong length or something.

'Course not. In fact, it's the opposite – I've got a proposition for you.'

'Proposition? What sort of a proposition?' My mind had gone into warp factor ten by this time.

'Look, come to the sixth-form block at twelve-thirty and I'll tell you all about it. But don't say anything to anyone yet. OK?'

'OK.' Confusion to the millionth degree! I hadn't a clue what I was letting myself in for.

'Ciao!' And off she went.

As I walked back along the corridor, Spud's tongue was almost dragging on the floor. 'What was all that about?'

'Dunno,' I said, truthfully.

'Aw, come on.'

'Honest! I don't know what it was about.'

'Well, what did she say?'

'Nothing much.'

'She must've said something.'

'Not really.'

'Ooooo! Dan, Dan, the secret man! What will Magenta say?'

And then, in Maths, he went and sat with Magnus and Angus Lyle, or the Liable Twins as they're called. Magnus is OK, in fact he can be quite cool, but I can't stand Angus – he's a total liability. Talk about two crystals short of a light sabre! So I sat on my own. I knew it was only jealousy on Spud's part but I was really pissed off with him. He *is* supposed to be my best mate, after all.

Anyway, as soon as the bell went at lunchtime I went round to the sixth-form block.

'Is Samantha Campion in?'

This boy called Darien Quinn answered the door. He played Romeo in last year's school play and talk about I'm in love with the face in the mirror! He fancies himself as some great Shakespearean actor and calls everyone 'dahling'. What a plonker.

'Sammy? Yeah, cool. Hold on.' He was so busy looking at his reflection in the glass panel of the door that he hardly looked at me. 'Hey, Sammy darling, there's a kid at the door for you!' Kid! *Cheek!* He's only three years older than me!

'My name's Samantha and I'm not your darling!' I heard Samantha shout as she came to the door. 'Hi, Dan, come in.' She was eating a Pot Noodle and I have to say she was quite pretty, so I could see what Spud was drooling about, but she wasn't a patch on my Magenta. 'Do you mind me calling you Dan?' she said as we picked our way across the orange peel and screwed-up paper on the floor. I'd never been in the sixth-form common room before and I was disappointed; it looked a bit of a doss house, if you ask me. There was a dart board with a strategically placed poster of Victoria Beckham, several empty Coke cans lying around, and enough magazines and tabloid newspapers to stock a modest-sized branch of WHSmith.

I have to admit, I love the way Magenta says my name, with a slightly elongated 'Da-aniel', but hey, who was I to argue with someone in Year 12?

'Dan's fine,' I said.

'Cool. OK, Dan, this is the thing. I've been appointed head of the stage crew for this year's production – we're doing *Grease* by the way – and we're recruiting new people.'

Last year when I went to watch *Romeo and Juliet*, I was more impressed with the stage crew sitting up in the box than I was with what was going on on the stage. Mum and I were sitting near the back and I could see that they had this mega desk in front of them and they were twiddling knobs and sliding buttons up and down when the lights changed or they needed a sound effect. I thought they were totally wicked. And at the interval they were all running about with headsets and looking really cool. But I wasn't sure why Samantha was talking to me about it because the stage crew's only open to Year 10 and above.

'Oh, good,' I said, trying to sound as mature and interested as I could. If I'm being honest I was feeling a bit weird in there because, for a start, I was the only person in school uniform. And anyway, I wasn't sure how I was supposed to respond.

'The thing is, quite a few of last year's stage crew have dropped out.' She took another mouthful of Pot Noodle and then waved her fork around in a sort of airy-fairy way. I started to watch it but then felt a bit dizzy, so stopped. 'They say that it's too much to put on a production at Easter when they've got exams in the summer.' I still wasn't sure where all this was leading. 'So, anyway, I was talking to some of the staff about it and Mr Behl suggested you.'

I thought I couldn't have heard her properly. 'Me?'

'Yeah, Dan, you.' She smiled this really cute smile. I mean, I didn't fancy her or anything like that – she might be year 12 but she was nowhere near as gorgeous as Magenta. 'He says you're showing real promise and even though you're still only Year 9, he thinks he'll be able to clear it with the Head, if you're interested.'

If I'm interested! Oh my God! Was Captain Kirk interested in intergalactic travel?

'Wow!' I couldn't believe I'd said that. What a nerd.

'So, I'll take that as a yes then, shall I?'

'Not some how!' Eeek! What a load of garbage was coming out of my mouth.

I was so excited I couldn't wait to tell Magenta. This was like a dream come true! Samantha started walking towards the door and I got the impression that our little meeting was over.

'You mustn't say anything yet, though,' she said. 'Mr Behl and I are going to see the Head on Monday and clear it with him. We don't want the whole school clamouring to get in that little box, do we?' She lobbed her empty Pot Noodle tub into the bin and scored a direct hit.

'OK, Campion, you've impressed me. You can be in the team.' Brett Carter, the captain of the basketball team, was just coming into the common room as we got to the door. I could tell that Samantha liked him because she started flicking her hair, the way girls do if they fancy someone. Then she leaned against the doorframe and started to laugh in this really flirty way. 'Anyway, I'm holding a meeting at my house tonight at seven-thirty for everyone in the technical crew. I want us to be a really tight team so I thought we'd do a bit of bonding over a pizza or something. Will you be able to make it?' She was talking to me but her eyes were following Brett Carter around.

Would I be able to make it? I'd kill to get there. 'Sure, I can be there,' I said nonchalantly. I couldn't wait to tell Magenta.

She wrote down her address on a piece of paper and gave her hair another flick. 'But don't forget, Dan, you mustn't mention this to anyone outside the stage crew until after Monday. You could get me into a whole heap of trouble, OK?'

'No problem!' What was I saying? Here I was bursting to tell Magenta and promising not to. Deception has never been my strong point and I thought I'd explode if I had to wait all weekend.

'So, see you tonight then. My place at about half-seven – OK?' She went back inside the sixth-form block and shut the door.

Yes! There was no one around and I punched the air as I dashed off to find Magenta. I was sure it wouldn't matter if I told just *her* – I mean, I'd swear her to secrecy and everything. But I couldn't find her anywhere. Spud was sulking and still hanging around with the Liable Twins so I was on my own, feeling like a man who'd won the lottery while sitting on a desert island.

All afternoon I was planning how I was going to tell her. I would taunt her a little bit and get her to tease it out of me a syllable at a time. I was so excited! When I got out of double Science I went to the door by the cloakroom where we always meet. I was a bit late because Angus Lyle had set light to the end of

Anju Patel's plait with his bunsen burner and the whole class had to stay behind and write out the 'Rules of the Laboratory' five times. By the time I got there I was practically busting a gut. But Magenta wasn't there.

'She's already left,' Seema said, between snogs with her new bloke, Hayden West.

Already left? How could she have already left? We've always walked home together, even before we were an item. I ran towards the gate and managed to catch up with her but she was in a right old strop. I tried to hold her hand but she snatched it away like I'd got the plague or something. I tried asking if she was upset but that just seemed to get her even more upset and then she started to go on about me not meeting her for lunch. This wasn't how it was supposed to be at all. In my head I'd told Magenta my news, even though I'd promised Samantha that I wouldn't say a thing, and she'd been really excited for me and had thrown her arms round me and we'd kissed and then spent the whole weekend sharing our secret. But now it was all going horribly wrong.

'Look,' I said, 'it's all a big secret but if you promise not to say anything . . .' but just as I was going to tell her, who should come down the driveway but Samantha Campion! Eeek! Caught in the act of betraying her trust! What a dilemma! I don't know how James Bond does it. I am definitely not cut out for a career in MI5.

'Hi, Dan!'

All I did was say 'Hi,' back but, for some reason, that seemed to be the final straw for Magenta. She stomped off, shouting about how we were finished and how I'd obviously prefer to be called Dan from now on.

'Well, that's women for you, mate.' Spud was giving me the benefit of his wealth of experience with girls – which is precisely zilch! He'd decided he'd had enough of Angus Lyle after Angus blamed him for the arson assault on Anju's hair. 'All I did was tell him how my sister Kerry said that girls used to burn off their split ends with a match and the next thing I know Anju's plait's gone up like a Roman candle and the whole lab stinks of singed hair. What a moron!'

I resisted the urge to say, it takes one to know one because, actually, I was quite pleased to have someone to talk to. 'I just don't understand. It's not like I didn't search the whole school for her, you know.'

'Once they've got you under their thumb, mate, that's where they want you to stay.'

'Magenta's not like that,' I argued.

'Believe me, you're better off without her.'

'No, I'm not.' I know I sounded like a wimp but I really don't believe that I *am* better off without her. I've been potty about her for so long, the last month has been like a dream come true.

'Trust me, mate, when I went out with her . . .'

That was it! 'Spud!' I shouted. 'You did *not* go out with her, OK? You forced a kiss on her and then got lip-locked for five hours. That does not constitute going out with somebody. Not even in the Desperately-Pathetic-Clutching-at-Straws Dictionary of Definitions!'

'OK, OK.' Spud looked really upset and I felt awful. 'So, you going to go for that Samantha chick, then?'

Suddenly I didn't feel awful any more. 'She is not a chick and I'm not going to go for her. I want to sort it out with Magenta.'

We were walking towards my house and Spud went silent. I was beginning to regret inviting him round. 'Well,' he said, after a while, 'why don't you give her a bit of time to cool off and then go round there tonight?'

'Brilliant!' And then I realised that I was supposed to be going to my first stage crew meeting. 'Oh, but I can't tonight. I've arranged to go out.'

'Where to?'

'Just out.'

'Can't you cancel?'

'Not really.'

'Where're you going? You didn't say anything about it before.' Spud was throwing more questions at me than Chris Tarrant. And I couldn't answer any of them without either lying or breaking my word. What a nightmare! Then his face lit up. 'You *are* seeing that Samantha chick, aren't you? You sly old thing!'

'Leave it out, Spud! I am *not* making a play for Samantha Campion.' We'd got to my house by now and I looked up at next door and saw Magenta at her bedroom window. She made a big show of drawing the curtains as we went up the path to my front door. She looked so sad and so lovely.

Spud started chanting, 'Daniel's telling porkies! Daniel's telling porkies!'

'Leave it out, Spud!' I thought that I might punch his lights out if he didn't shut up.

As we went in, I saw an envelope on the doormat. It was hand-written and addressed to the whole family, so I opened it.

Dad's girlfriend thing around Art. In Art I'm practically guaranteed an A* because (I don't mean to brag here but let's be honest) I do have a huge wodge of natural talent. Whereas in Geography, I have zero talent and would be lucky to scrape a C. I think last week's lesson clinched it really. Mr Kingston was talking about climatic changes and I just made one little comment about 'the big blue country to the north of Africa,' and the whole class went into terminal hysteria. I mean, how was I supposed to know the difference between a land mass and the Mediterranean? So after that I started thinking: A* or C? Let's think. Erm – no contest really.

But then, no sooner had I given the great Blob my glad tidings than there was a teensy bit of a hiccup. You see, this term in Art we've been developing our clay work. Ms 'Lovely' Lovell (who can do no wrong in my father's eyes – yuk, yuk!) wanted everyone to produce at least one pot that they'd thrown on the wheel. I'd been putting it off but this morning it was my turn.

'Pat the clay into a ball, Magenta – like this,' she said – as if I didn't know how to make a ball of clay.

'Thank you, Ms Lovell, I can manage.' I banged the clay into the middle of the wheel. She likes her students to call her Belinda when we're in her lessons but, to be quite honest, it doesn't seem right to me. I mean, she is a teacher after all – even if she *is* going out with my dad, and I don't think teachers should get so cosy and pally with their pupils – it's not right. So there was no way I was going to let her get all matey in the studio in front of everyone. It was bad enough that everyone knows that she comes to my house in the evenings and at weekends. I mean, a girl in my situation does need to maintain a certain degree of credibility, right?

'OK, now put a little water over it and as you gently press the pedal with your foot, wrap your hands round the clay with your thumbs on top and centre it – like this.' And she only went and put her hands right over the top of mine! Can you believe it?

'Whoa!' I pulled my hands away. I thought it was supposed to be against the law for teachers to make physical contact with pupils. 'Ms Lovell, can I speak to you outside for a moment, please?'

But, when we got into the corridor, I was just about to tell her to back off, when she turned on *me*. I mean, I've been in her group since Year 7 and I've never seen her get mad – ever! Not even when Billy O'Dowd did rude things with the still life arrangement last year. But she was furious!

'That is it, Magenta! I've had enough!' I was shocked. I don't know what *she'd* had enough of – after all, *I* was the one who'd been manhandled over the potter's wheel. 'I know the current situation can't be easy for you but it isn't easy for me either.' Pul-ease! How was it not easy for her? Had one of *her* teachers completely invaded *her* life? I don't think so! 'And I'm not going to tolerate your attitude any longer.'

'*What* attitude?'

'Most of the time you ignore me and when you do speak you're rude.'

It seemed to me that I couldn't win: I don't speak to her, I'm wrong; I do speak to her, I'm wrong. See – lose, lose! 'Me being rude?' She was the one treating me like I didn't know how to put a lump of clay on to a wheel. I mean, how difficult could it be, for heavens' sake?

'Yes, rude, Magenta. And I'm not standing for it any longer. I'm going to see Mrs Delaney first thing tomorrow to ask that you be transferred into Mrs Joshua's group as from next week.'

Aggh! Not Mrs Joshua! Her lessons were about as enjoyable as a prison camp. Whenever I've had to take notes to her it's been like walking into a morgue. There's no radio and no one's allowed to talk. You can recognise classes on their way to her lessons because they look about as happy as a herd of constipated elephants. And the worst thing is, their artwork has all the creativity of painting by numbers. Belinda might be a lot of things but at least she believes in freedom of expression – or at least she had done until recently.

'Now, Magenta, I need time to calm down a bit so I don't want you to come back into the lesson.' Honestly – how pathetic was that? And to think I used to believe she was cool! I can only imagine that some of my dad's bad habits have been rubbing off on her. 'And, unless you want to fail this assignment, you'd better find time either at lunchtime or after school to throw your pot before the firing on Friday. OK?'

'Yes, Ms Lovell.' I gave a big, irritated *humph* so that she knew exactly how petty I thought she was being.

But it's typical, isn't it? I'd only just made my decision to take Art, on the grounds that I was pretty sure of a good grade, when Belinda Lovell goes and threatens me with relegation to the dregs group. If that happened I could kiss goodbye to any hope of an A*. In fact, it was more than likely that Sirius would be producing better work than me by the time my exam came round. I was feeling pretty peed off actually and was wondering how I was:

a) going to get round Belinda without having to apologise for something I hadn't done and

b) going to get my pot thrown before Friday.

And then it occurred to me that if I solved the second problem, the first one would probably sort itself out. I know I moan about my dad going out with my teacher and everything but, suddenly, I could see how I might be able to make it work to my advantage. My dad's an artist, right? (Well, a graphic designer, which is pretty close.) And he really wants me to take Art so, provided that I didn't give Belinda any grounds to throw me out, I was sure I could get Dad to talk her round and snatch my future out of the jaws of Mrs Joshua.

It was beautifully simple really. Now all I had to do was to throw my pot before Friday. And the more I thought about it, the more it seemed to me that *throwing* a pot was not the problem – as I said before, just how hard can it be? The real problem was *where* I was going to throw it. One thing was certain, there was no way I was going to give Belinda the satisfaction of teaching me on a one-to-one basis. I was going to have to find either another teacher or another venue – or both.

At our school the Art department is in the same block as some of the Technology rooms and I was wandering up and down the corridor, giving the old neurones a run for their money, when I just happened to look into one of the workshops. And I had a brainwave! There was a Year 10 group in there and this boy called Ryan Dunn (who only arrived at our school at the end of last term after he'd got kicked out of Leonardo da Vinci) was at the bench right next to the window. He's quite cool and loads of girls fancy him. (I have to say, he didn't look quite so hot with his plastic goggles on, but he was still OK.) They were doing some sort of electronics and I was watching him messing around with this spinning turntable – and that's when my brainwave happened.

Ryan looked up and saw me watching him. He pushed his goggles up on top of his head, you know, like old-fashioned pilots used to do, and he smiled at me. He looked really masculine actually. I mean, he still had red dents across his nose and round his eyes where the goggles had pressed in but, apart from that, he looked really cute. I gave him one of my best smiles – I've been practising in front of my bedroom mirror so that I can get it just right. Hardly any teeth showing – just a little curl of the lips. It's not about hiding my brace or anything like that, it's supposed to be alluring according to this magazine article I was reading. Then you have to give a slight raise of the eyebrows. Wow – it obviously worked because he winked at me! How brilliant was that? Sadly there'd been no one to see it – except Mr Behl, who shouted at Ryan to get on with his work and waved me out of the way.

But still, I'd got two things from my little stroll along the corridor:

1) a boost to my self confidence, (which had taken a bit of a knock after the whole Daniel two-timing episode) and also,

2) it'd given me a solution to my problem. Excellent!

Add to that the fact that standing outside had meant I'd got out of clearing up the Art room at the end of the lesson and I was feeling pretty pleased with myself as we went to our next lesson, which was Drama. I was telling Arlette all about Ryan and my plan to get my pot made when, suddenly, I stopped dead in my tracks. Standing in front of us was the most gorgeous boy I think I've ever seen. He was in the corridor outside the Performing Arts department – like a vision in denim with a bandanna round his forehead. I mean, how arty is *that?*

I grabbed Arlette's arm. 'Oh my God, Arl! He is *so* gorgeous!'

'What? Him!' To be honest I'd expected a little more enthusiasm, but I suppose she is *in lurve* with Ben at the moment. Although that's a whole other issue. I do wonder about Arlette's self respect sometimes. I mean, Ben is Seema's ex – so it's like she's snogging her friend's cast-off if you think about it. Talk about second-hand goods!

But leaving Arlette's love life aside. 'Do you know him then?'

'Know *of* him. Didn't you see the school play last year? Oh no, I'd forgotten.'

I'd boycotted last year's production of *Romeo and Juliet* for reasons of conscience. Mr Grimsby, my teacher in Year 8 and head of Drama, had told Dad at the parents' evening that my acting ability made the *Carry On* team look like the Royal Shakespeare Company. Cheek! And that I'd do better to get under the skin of the character I was playing rather than trying to make each character act like the head of the mod squad. Honestly! Just because, when we were doing an exercise about status and power and he wanted me to play a road sweeper to Janet Dibner's executive business woman I argued, quite reasonably, that my road sweeper was a former

40

captain of industry who'd fallen on hard times. I mean, the teachers are always telling us to avoid stereotypical judgements but when we do, look what happens. So anyway I thought it would've been pretty hypocritical if I'd gone to one of the Grim Reaper's productions. I mean, how could I have lived with myself if I'd supported something that was run by a man who seemed to derive pleasure and satisfaction from the destruction of creative talent?

But, to get back to the hunk in the headgear. 'Was he in it then?'

'In it? You'd've thought he was up for an Oscar.' Arlette can be quite cutting at times. 'Apparently his mum was some famous actress and he goes on about it all the time.'

'The son of a famous actress? How exciting.' I went over to the notice board where he was standing and I saw that he was reading the list where people had signed up for the auditions for this year's play. 'Ooo, *Grease*!' I was looking at the photographs of John Travolta and Olivia Newton John that were stuck all over the notice board. 'That sounds better than Shakespeare.'

He looked at me and gave me this really sweet smile before he walked off. That was two gorgeous guys smiling at me in the space of ten minutes! Boy, am I using the right toothpaste, or what? 'What's his name, Arl?' I said, staring at the ream of names on the list.

'I think that's him,' she said, pointing to the very first name.

'Darien Quinn. Ooo! Can't you just tell his mother's an actress with a name like Darien? And he's going for the lead role of Danny.' Then I had another absolutely brilliant brainwave. (I mean is this the season for them or what? It must be Gran's cooking – although, when I think of the charred remains of her pasta bake last night, maybe not.) I took out my pen and wrote mine, Arlette's and Seema's names up on the list for auditions. Seema had been out all morning taking her grade six piano exam (honestly, I sometimes wonder if there's anything she *can't* do), but I was sure she wouldn't mind.

Arlette didn't seem too keen on the idea though. 'What're you doing?'

'It'll be so fantastic. It'll be fun.' I could see it now; I'd be Sandra Dee and I'd have to kiss Darien. And Arlette and Seema could be the Pink Ladies. I could hardly wait – it would be wicked.

'We're going to be late!' Arlette walked towards the Drama studio and I got the impression that she was in a bit of a huff. So I left it at that.

Then, when Seema came back at lunchtime, I was filling her in on what had happened. 'Oh, I can't tell you how fabulous he is.' I was describing Darien. '*And* he's mature.' Which was one of the most attractive things about him actually – it's so refreshing to find maturity in a boy these days. Mind you, he *is* in the sixth form, which could account for it.

'He didn't smile *at* you, Magenta. He was smiling at what you said.' I don't know what was eating Arlette but she was turning into Mrs McNitty of Gritty. 'You know, when you said, "*Grease* would be better than Shakespeare."?'

'So, what's your point, Arlette?'

'My point is, he's in Year 12 so there's no way he'd be smiling at you in *that* way.' It was quite obvious that Arlette was jealous – maybe she fancied Darien Quinn too?

'Well, Daniel's throwing himself at some slapper Year 12 girl, so I don't see why it's any different for me.' I could feel myself getting peed off, thank goodness Seema interrupted.

'I don't think age has got anything to do with it,' she said. 'In fact I think that it's far better if relationships are based on like-mindedness.'

Oh, Seema's so wise. I sometimes wish I was her. And actually, I agree with her. Take my cousin

Justine, for example. She's three months older than I am, so you would think she'd be three months more mature, right? But no way! We are miles apart in terms of maturity and sophistication. For example, her fashion sense is so nineties it's practically retro (notice I said 'practically') and her conversational skills can just about stretch from 'West' to 'Life' but the teensiest deviation and she's totally out of her depth. So, really, if Justine was looking for a potential boyfriend, although she's almost fourteen, she'd be better off looking at twelve year olds if she wanted to get an equal match in terms of maturity. Whereas I, on the other hand, have the experiences and interests that are more in line with boys who're two and even three years older than I am. So it's completely understandable that a sixth-former would be interested in me. I really didn't get why Arlette had the hump.

'Is something bugging you, Arlette?' Seema asked. 'You've seemed really off all lunchtime.'

'Yes, there is, actually.' And she glared at me. I couldn't believe it. What was I supposed to have done?

But I decided to be an adult about it. 'Look, if it's something I've said, I want you to tell me about it, OK?' See what I mean about maturity?

'You just signed my name up for an audition without even asking!' Arlette blurted out. Wow, talk about touchy.

'I'm sorry.' I couldn't see what the big deal was – the three of us always did things together. And anyway she could always say no.

But then she explained and it turns out Arlette had had a traumatic experience when she was nine. She'd been playing Marta in their church's production of *The Sound of Music* when Captain von Trapp had accidentally trodden on her skirt and ripped it off. She'd been left standing on stage in her knickers with everyone laughing at her. Poor Arlette had been scarred for life.

'Oh, Arl, I'm sorry. You should've said.' I put my arm round her. 'We'll go and cross off your name this minute.'

'No – then you and Seema will get in and you'll be off at rehearsals all the time and I'll be left on my own.' She did have a point. What a dilemma.

Anyway, Seema and I promised that we'd make sure nothing traumatic like that happened again and luckily Seema was totally up for the auditions. The first round is tomorrow after school – I can hardly wait. Ooo, it's going to be so fantastic. The only thing is, that means I've only got tonight to get my pot thrown with my new plan. And then afterwards, I'll have to watch the video of *Grease* a few times so that I can get into character like Mr Grimsby said I should.

'Are you sure this is going to work?' Arlette had come home with me but, having got over the whole auditions trauma, she was being a total wuss about Operation Potter's Wheel.

'Why *shouldn't* it work? Sssh.' I stood still in the hall and listened. 'Gran!' There was no answer. 'Brilliant! We can get this finished and cleared up before anyone's home and then Belinda will have to take back all the horrible things she's said about me.'

'What horrible things has she said about you?'

I sometimes wonder what planet Arlette's on. 'All that stuff about moving me into Mrs Joshua's group. That's pretty horrible.'

'Well, not really. She only said it cos you were being off with her.'

'Me? Off with her?' I couldn't believe what I was hearing.

'Look, Madge, let's just leave it and get on with this, can we? I've got to get home or Mum'll go spare.'

Arlette hardly ever comes round these days. We

used to practically live in each other's houses but that's all died out recently. 'Why don't you give her a ring and tell her you're going to eat here? You could even sleep over – like we used to.'

She looked really guilty. 'Thanks, but it's OK.' Then she started to get twitchy. 'Come on, let's just get this over with.'

I mean, it was all right for her: she'd already made a mug that she was going to give to her mum for Mother's Day and, also, her entire future wasn't hanging on this assignment!

'Chill, will you?' I dumped my bag and coat in the hall. 'Right, the clay's in my bag. You get that out and I'll bring Dad's record player through from the sitting room.'

As I'd been watching Ryan in the workshop, it'd occurred to me that all I needed was something that went round like a potter's wheel and I'd be able to make my pot at home and then present it to Belinda for firing before Friday. It was so simple; it was brilliant! Am I a genius, or what?

Arlette unwrapped the lump of clay that I'd put in a plastic bag and I set up Dad's record player on the kitchen table. 'OK, let's get this baby thrown.' I was so pleased with my idea. I banged the clay into the middle of the turntable on top of the little metal bit that holds the record in place. 'Do you think it matters that there'll be a hole in the bottom?'

Arlette shrugged. 'I don't know, but I think you should take the rubber mat off. There'll be too much friction otherwise.' You see: that's why two brains are better than one. I was so glad she'd come to help me.

I lifted the clay off again but the slip mat was already covered with brown gunk. 'Oops! We'd better wash that before Dad gets back.' I tossed it towards the sink but Sirius did his frisbee-style party piece and grabbed it mid-air, then ran off under the table. 'Leave, Sirius! Leave!' For a little dog, Sirius has got remarkably strong jaws and by the time I managed to extricate it from between his teeth it looked like a black rubber doily.

'I really don't think this is a good idea, you know.' Honestly, Arlette's got no bottle.

'Don't worry. I'll ask Joe. . .' I had been going to say 'Daniel' but then I remembered that I wasn't speaking to him, '. . . to get me a new one.' I sat down at the table again. 'Right. Now, let's get this thing going. What do I do next?'

'First of all you've got to get it spinning,' Arlette said.

Now, Dad's record player is practically an antique and the only way to start the turntable rotating was to move the stylus arm across to the middle. Problem! There was a dirty great lump of clay in the way. It was obvious that this was going to be a two-person job. 'I'll squish the clay down a bit while you lift the needle over the top, OK?' But just as I was saying it Arlette got a bit too keen and rammed the needle into the back of my hand. 'Ouch!' I jumped back with the shock. There was a sickening snap of plastic and the arm of Dad's record player went swinging over the edge of the table, dangling by a couple of wires.

'Oh my God, Magenta! Your dad's going to kill us!'

'*Us?*' I like the way Arlette always tries to dump the blame. '*You* were the one who stabbed me with the needle.'

'Well, it was your stupid idea!'

The last thing we needed was a slanging match so I tried to calm her down a bit. 'Look, don't worry. Dad hardly ever uses this any more. He just plays CDs most of the time. I'll pop it round to Joe to get it mended and he'll never notice. Trust me.'

'But what if he does?'

'Well . . .' I looked at Sirius and had an idea. '. . . I'll just tell him Sirius did it. Anyway, let's look on the bright side – at least we can switch it on without the arm hitting the clay now.' I clicked the little stump of plastic over to the middle and the turntable started to go round. Yes! It was working. The clay looked a bit like a drunken jelly, wobbling round and round but it was pretty wicked. It's so rewarding to see one's ideas come to fruition, don't you think? 'Excellent! So, what's next?' I was getting quite excited.

'You need to moisten the clay a bit.' Arlette was still faffing about with the broken arm of the record player so I filled a jug of water from the sink and began to dribble it over the clay.

Suddenly Arlette looked up and screamed. 'No – Madge!'

'*Ow!*' I nearly jumped out of my skin. There was this incredible blue flash and a huge bang. The turntable had been spinning round but it gradually petered out. At the same time the fridge shuddered and stopped. 'Ooops! That was a close one.'

'A close one?' Arlette's voice was trembling and she looked pretty near to tears actually. 'Are you mental? It's a miracle we're not both dead!'

'Er, slight exaggeration, I think.' Trust Arlette to over-react.

'Oh really? So when we were doing conduction

of electricity last term, exactly *which* part of the whole "water plus electricity equals death-by-frying" equation did you not get?'

Oooo, talk about sarcasm. And doesn't it just prove my point about her always trying to wriggle out of stuff? 'Well, *you* were the one who said to moisten the clay,' I pointed out.

'Yes, moisten! Not saturate it so that it looked like some Charlie Dimmock ornamental water feature!' (Did I say earlier that I was pleased Arlette had come home with me? Well, reverse that.) 'Now you've not only ruined your dad's record player but you've blown all the fuses as well. And look at my jumper!'

Honestly there were a few splashes, that was all. 'That'll wash out, no worries.'

'Yes worries, Magenta. Look, this was a very bad idea and I want out of here! I'm not staying around to witness what happens when your dad gets home. One explosion's enough for me, thank you.'

'No, Arl – wait a minute.' No way was she going to desert me at this point. 'You've got to help me get the electricity back on!' She did much better than me in Science – come to think of it, *everybody* did much better than me in Science. 'Please, Arl. I'm sorry, OK?

Perhaps I got a bit carried away about the whole turntable/potter's wheel thing. If you sort out the fuses, I'll clear up this mess.'

'And you'll go into the studio at lunchtime tomorrow to do your pot?'

Gggrr! 'OK.'

'Promise?'

'I promise.'

Anyway, so we were under the stairs, me holding the torch while Arlette pushed the fuse back in, when something caught my eye. Dad's electric drill and sanding disc – you know, that circular thing that goes on the front of a drill and then sandpaper attaches to it? Of course! Why hadn't I thought of it before? It would be much easier than the stupid record player because we could put the clay on the disc part (without the sandpaper, obviously) and wrap a plastic bag round the body of the drill to protect the electrical bits. Then, if we wedged it in the drawer of the kitchen table, it would stay upright and I'd be able to throw my pot. Perfect!

'No way!'

'Oh, come on, Arlette – I need you to show me what to do.'

'No! Absolutely not! I'm going home.'

* * *

It actually took longer than we thought to make the whole thing watertight. You wouldn't believe how many sandwich bags we used but in the end I was pretty confident that no water could get inside. We opened the drawer of the table and put the drill in it so that the disc was more or less horizontal and then Arlette held the drawer in place with one hand and was ready to push the start button of the drill with the other. I'd got the clay fairly wet before I slammed it on to the middle of the disc this time, just so that we didn't have a repeat performance. Gran always says making mistakes is a good thing because you learn from them. (I wonder if that's why her cooking's so awful – because she thinks that if she makes enough mistakes, one day she'll wake up as Delia Smith?)

'Ready?' I said to Arlette.

'Not really.'

'Don't worry about it. It'll be OK,' I tried to reassure her. 'So, when you press the button, I'm going to put my hands round the clay and start pressing it evenly till it's centred – is that right?'

'Yes – I think so.' Arlette was crouched down, pushing in the drawer at arm's length.

'OK. Three, two . . .'

'How about if I wear your gran's rubber gloves and a pair of wellies?'

'Trust me, Arlette. We are not going to get electrocuted. Just chill.' I took a deep breath. 'Go!'

Then suddenly everything seemed to happen at once. As soon as Arlette pressed the start button the drill went into overdrive. It started spinning at about a thousand revs a second. There was no way I could get my hands anywhere near the clay to centre it, it was going so fast. In fact, the clay was doing the complete opposite of centring – it was shooting off the disc in every direction and spraying all over the kitchen like some sort of muddy Catherine wheel.

'Aaaagh!' Arlette screamed and leapt out of the way. The good side of that was that once she'd let go of the button, the drill slowed down and stopped. On the other hand, as she dived sideways she let go of the drawer so that the drill slipped over into the vertical position and flung the last remnants of clay on to the ceiling and all across the floor. She'd also managed to step on Sirius in the process and he started yelping and scuttling round the kitchen, getting more and more splattered in gunge.

I couldn't believe it; it looked as though the kitchen had been completely redecorated in brown polka dots by some Iron Age wattle-and-daub interior designer – the walls, the floor, the ceiling – even the light switch. There wasn't a surface that had escaped. And every single appliance, from the fridge to the salt and pepper pots, was speckled with mud. Even Sirius looked like one of those chocolate animals you get at Easter.

I looked at Arlette and caught a glimpse of my own reflection in what little bit of Gran's mirror was still visible. What a mess we looked. Clay was splattered on our faces and in our hair; not to mention our uniforms looking as though they'd been trailed across several acres of farmland in a rainstorm. Now, if you think *my* dad's a rageaholic, you should meet Arlette's parents. They are not exactly famous for their open-mindedness when it comes to freak accidents like this. So my mind was already racing ahead, trying to think of either:

a) a plan to get both us and the house cleaned up before parental wrath could descend from any direction – which, to be honest, was going to require nothing short of an army of superheroes with several thousand tankers of liquid cleaner, or, more realistically,

b) a plausible lie to explain what'd happened (not that I'm condoning lying, you understand, but in the circumstances it seemed like the only alternative to Arlette and me having a suicide pact).

'Now look what you've done!' Arlette looked at me like some mutinous mud-wrestler.

'*Me!* What about *you*?' Honestly – I rest my case.

Then, before I knew what was happening, she stood up, scraped a handful of clay off the table and slung it straight at me.

'I don't know why I ever listen to you, Magenta! My mum and dad are right – you *are* a bad influence!'

I couldn't believe what I was hearing. Me, a bad influence? How could anybody think that? But before I could say anything—

'What on earth!' Uh-oh! Dad was home.

'Magenta?' And he was accompanied by the root of all my problems – Belinda.

Suddenly it seemed like three really important things in my life were at stake here:

1) my place in Belinda's Art group so that I could get a decent grade,

2) a chance to impress both Darien and Mr Grimsby at tomorrow's audition, and, most importantly,

3) my friendship with Arlette.

I had the uneasy feeling that it was going to

require either a miracle or some pretty quick thinking if I was going to salvage any one of them. There was nothing for it. Desperate situations require desperate remedies, as they say. I was going to have to resort to playing my trump card: I was going to have to tell the truth!

4
Daniel

OK, check this out – Magenta and I are going to get
back together!

There's just one small problem though – well, two
small problems really:
1) Magenta doesn't know yet and
2) I'm not sure how to let her know. It's a bit tricky
   getting over a communications breakdown when
   we're still not communicating.

So, you're probably wondering how I know we're
going to get back together? Well, Curtis came round
and told Mum that the whole dumping thing was a
humungous mix up on the communications front.
And – wait for this – Magenta's really upset about it!
Is that amazing news, or is that amazing news? I'm
so relieved. This last week has been one of the worst
weeks of my life; even worse than when I got mumps
while I was staying at Dad's and Joe and I had to
stay there for nearly ten days and share a bedroom.

Anyway, there I was, on the settee, debating
whether to go to bed or stay where I was watching

this mindless chat show on cable. Well, when I say watching, I mean numbing out in front of it. At least I was relatively pain-free after a whole week of having to put up with the 'talk to the hand' policy that Magenta's been adopting. And she hadn't been exactly open to home visits either – she's had her curtains drawn all week with a notice stuck to the window saying, 'SCUMBAGS GO AWAY (that means you Daniel)'.

So I was lying there, feeling pretty miserable but knowing that if I went up to my bedroom I'd feel even worse because I'd either just lie there staring up at Sarah Michelle Gellar with thoughts bombing round my head like Michael Schumacher on turbo-drive; or if I put some music on, every track would remind me of Magenta and all the fantastic times we had together over Christmas. What a choice; insanity or depression! So, you know how they say; if in doubt, do nothing? Well, that's just what I'd decided – to do nothing – when the doorbell rang.

'Will one of you get that?' Mum was in the kitchen and it was obvious that my rodent-brother wasn't going to put himself out and come downstairs, so I went. I was a bit shocked because, standing on our doorstep, looking like a man who'd just lost everything, was Curtis.

'Hello, Daniel. Is your mother around?' He said he'd come round to talk to Mum about arrangements for his party but it didn't take a degree in psychology to work out that a man who looks that bad must have had another reason. I thought at first maybe Ms Lovell had dumped him – in which case I would've completely sympathised with him. Apart from the obvious parallel with me and the whole Magenta thing, I think Ms Lovell is really cool. I used to think it would be great if Curtis and Mum got it together. I had it all planned – we could've knocked a door through between the two houses and all lived together like the *Brady Bunch*. (We might've had to put Joe up for adoption to complete the happy family scenario but I could've lived with that.) But then, as I got older, I realised that that would've made Magenta my stepsister – which is a whole area I don't even want to think about. So when I found out about Curtis and Ms Lovell, I was really pleased. I think they make a fantastic couple and if they'd finished I'd be the first to commiserate with Curtis.

Anyway, I led Curtis through to the kitchen and went back into the living room. We've got one of those serving hatches between our kitchen and the through-lounge, so it doesn't exactly require NATO intelligence equipment to earwig on what's being said in the next room. I didn't want to turn the volume down too low in case Mum cottoned on to what I was doing, so I had to strain a bit to hear above the telly, but it sounded as though Curtis was keeping up the front about the party.

'Well, any way we can help out, just let us know.' Mum was going along with the party thing – although I didn't like the way she was saying *we* and *us* – I had an uneasy feeling that I was going to get lumbered. I was still convinced that there was more to this than Curtis was letting on, so I went over and crouched down under the hatch.

They were talking about sleeping arrangements – apparently Curtis' brother and his family are coming down for the whole of half-term week to help with the preparations.

'I wondered if Holden could come and sleep round here with one of the boys? You know, all lads together.'

Oh and I wonder which 'one of the boys' that would be! I can see Joe volunteering to share his passion-pad with an eight year old.

'No problem. I'm sure Daniel wouldn't mind.' Didn't I say I'd get lumbered? But just when I was on the point of bursting in and objecting to having to spend my half-term babysitting, the conversation started to get juicy.

'How's he bearing up?'

'What? Over the break-up?' My ears suddenly became Mr Spock-like antennae. 'Pretty miserable.' Cheers, Mum! Why do parents do that? Doesn't my credibility mean anything to her? 'How about Magenta?' Now this was the part I'd been waiting to hear.

Curtis sighed. 'Oh, you know Magenta. She's putting on a brave face but actually she seems pretty cut up about it. She even said she wanted us to move to Cornwall.'

'Cornwall?'

Cornwall! I couldn't bear to think about life without Magenta just the other side of the wall – let alone hundreds of miles away. This was getting serious.

'But that seems to have blown over now . . .' Phew! 'And then tonight . . . you are not going to believe what she got up to tonight.'

I knew it – didn't I say there was something bothering Curtis? I was torn – part of me wanted to run up to my bedroom and get the electronics kit Dad had bought me for my eleventh birthday because it had a mini microphone in it, but the other part of me was aching to hear news of Magenta.

'She's got herself into a right old state about

things . . .' Oh, poor Magenta! I would've helped her to sort out her problems, if only she'd confided in me the way she used to. I craned my neck to hear but I think I must have misheard him because it sounded as though he was saying that Magenta had been trying to throw a pot using his record player and an electric sander. Nah! Can't be right. I knew I should've gone and got my mini microphone.

'Anyway, Belinda and I took Arlette home and talked to her parents about what'd happened while Mum supervised Magenta washing down the kitchen. Course, it's going to need redecorating before the party.'

'Sure. Poor Magenta! It must be such a worry for you, Curtis.'

'Oh, Mary, I'm at the end of my tether sometimes. All this stuff came out about her SATs and Belinda – and I think the break-up with Daniel was just about the final straw.' Yes! This was music to my ears. She was regretting it. Yes! Yes! Yes! There was hope.

'Did you ever find out what'd happened?' This was the crucial part.

'She seems to think that Daniel was two-timing her.' What! I couldn't believe what I was hearing. Spud – it had to be! The double crossing toe-rag! He must've filled her head with ideas about me and

Samantha, just so that he could try his luck again. Wait till I got hold of him tomorrow.

'Daniel? No, I don't believe it.' Good old Mum. I knew I could rely on her for my defence. 'Now if it was Joe we were talking about, I could understand it – but not Daniel.' How well she knows her sons.

'That's what I thought. I mean, you know I tend to be a bit protective of Magenta . . .' A bit? 'But I was pretty sure she was safe with Daniel and then it seems she saw him with another girl but he's denying it.'

This was too much! First of all, we were back to the *safe* factor again and, secondly, I hadn't denied anything because I hadn't been asked anything! Still, on the positive side, it explained what was going on and that it was simply a misunderstanding. And, if Magenta was as upset as Curtis was implying, then we'd be able to sort everything out and be back together in no time. I was so excited. It was the best news I'd had since Samantha told me that the Crusher had given the OK to me being in the stage crew.

But good things never last, do they? Just then Joe walked in and I could tell from the evil glint in his eye that he wasn't going to back me on my spying mission.

'Hey Mum!' he called.

'Ssssh!' But I should've known better than to even try.

'I think we've got woodworm. Oh no – it's another type of boring insect!' And he started poking his finger into my arm and twisting it like he was trying to drill down to the bone. 'Get it, bruv? A woodworm bores its way into wood.' Then he stopped drilling my arm and gave my ear a very painful flick. 'But you're just plain boring.'

'Very punny.' I stood up.

Unfortunately, just at that moment Mum opened the doors of the hatch. 'Did you call?'

'Ouch!'

'Oh, Daniel, darling. What on earth were you doing down there?'

My head felt like someone had stuck a chisel in my skull but I decided to be a man about it. Joe, meanwhile, was nearly wetting himself with delight. He vaulted over the back of the settee and sat there with his arms folded. 'Good one, Mum. Keep it up and you might knock some sense into him one day.'

I started to think of all the cruel, yet satisfying things I could do to him to get my revenge and I suddenly began to see all sorts of advantages to having Magenta's snotty little cousin staying in my room.

'Leave him be, Joe. And just show some respect for the furniture, will you. Come through, Daniel, love and I'll put some ice on it.'

Joe started to do his Ali G impression saying, 'Risspeck, man,' to the back of the sofa, but I left him to it.

Later on, when I was in bed with a bag of frozen peas on my head (to try and take the bump down so that I didn't look like a cartoon character that'd been hit with an anvil), Mum knocked on my door. I'd been lying there trying to solve the knotty little problem of how I could sort out the Magenta situation if she continued with her policy of non-cooperation, but also feeling very excited that my period of excommunication would soon be over.

'Can I come in?' Mum always asks but never actually waits for a reply. 'How's your head?'

'Still there, last time I looked in the mirror.'

'Give me the peas, love. You shouldn't keep them on for too long.'

'They're not really cold any more.' I said, tossing the mushy packet at her. Then I had a thought. 'Mum?'

'Yes, love.'

'You were a girl once, weren't you?'

She grinned in that sweet, maternal sort of way that makes me realize I've said something incredibly stupid and if I'd said it to anyone but my mother, I'd have been sentenced to several years of penal ridicule. 'Well, let's see, it says *female* on my birth certificate and I haven't had any major surgery since then, so yes, I think we can safely say I used to be a girl.' She came and sat down on the end of my bed. 'Is this a Magenta question?'

'No.' Don't you just hate it when you're so transparent? 'It's just a girls-in-general question.'

'OK. I'm all ears.'

'Well, if you'd broken up with someone because you thought they'd done something wrong and you were really upset about it but, actually, they hadn't really done it, wouldn't you want to know the truth?'

'Yes.' Then she sat there as if she was expecting something more.

'So how would the person you broke up with go about making sure you found out the truth if you won't speak to them?'

'Well, let's see, if I was a girl who suspected that someone she cared about . . .' (Cared about was OK – fancied passionately would've been better, but I'd go with cared about.) '. . . had cheated on her, then I think I'd be hurting quite a lot.'

I was getting impatient. 'Yes, so how can the person she cares about stop her hurting?'

'Well, you know, some girls will tell you that they like the strong macho types who come along and whisk them off their feet . . .' Strong and macho! Eeek! This could be a real sticking point. 'On the other hand . . .' Thank goodness: there was an *other hand*. I didn't think I was in with a chance if it was all down to strong and macho – '. . . some girls will tell you they want a man who's sensitive and caring and sharing . . .' Excellent, because I think I measure up quite well on the caring-sharing scale. 'But . . .' Uh oh – this was a *but* I didn't want – just when I was thinking I had the winning ticket – '. . . in actual fact, I don't think you can go far wrong if you hit a happy medium somewhere between the two.' She'd totally lost me now. 'Most girls do want someone who's kind and compassionate and who respects them; but they also want someone with a bit of oomph.' Oomph? What was *oomph* when it was at home? And more importantly, where could I get it? 'They want someone who's going to show a bit of initiative – a bit of romantic spontaneity – and be compassionate as well.'

I felt thoroughly depressed. It sounded as though having a successful relationship was going to require nothing short of red Y-fronts and a cape! 'So how would someone with oomph explain that they haven't done anything wrong so that the person who cares about them will go out with them again?'

'Same as always, love.' She kissed me on the forehead and started to leave the room. 'Tell the truth and be yourself. Now go to sleep and stop worrying. Any girl who doesn't fall madly in love with you wants her head testing. Night!'

'Night!' I wished I hadn't said anything. She'd been no help whatsoever.

Oomph? Did I have oomph? And if I did, how would I know? And if I didn't, was it something I could acquire? I think I was in danger of going into Michael Schumacher mode again.

On the positive side, Mum had definitely implied that Magenta cared about me and I'd heard Curtis with my own ears saying she was cut up about our break-up. So all I had to do now was use my initiative, be spontaneous and muster up all my oomph to tell her the truth. Humph – and all that without even a crystal of kryptonite. Why does life have to be so hard?

* * *

Talk about lousy timing. Last night I'd got the distinct impression that Mum was on my side, but this morning it was like she was out to totally sabotage me. For starters, I was sitting by my window, waiting for Magenta to leave the house so that I could dash down and just happen to be leaving at the same time (full marks for both initiative and spontaneity, I thought), when Mum suddenly went into one about the state of the bathroom. And my dearly beloved brother, who wouldn't know the truth if a polygraph came up and strapped itself to his rapidly expanding nose, looked her straight in the eye and resorted to his universal policy of 'deny everything'.

'It wasn't me.' I mean, how could she believe him? It so obviously *was* him. Even his scummy boxers were in the middle of the floor. 'Daniel was in there last.'

So all my plans about walking to school with Magenta went by the board because I was cleaning Joe's tide-mark off the bath. Ugh! Gross! By the time I got to school, she was going in through the gates. Great, I thought – just in time! And I was about to call out to her when I heard Mr Onanije, the deputy head, shout out, 'No skateboards in school, Dunn. Get off it now.'

Oh great! Ryan Dunn was skating down the road.

As soon as Mr Onanije shouted at him, he rotated on his back wheels so that he was going backwards, then as he caught up with Magenta, he leapt off, flicked the tail and caught the nose with one hand. How puke-provoking was that? You should've seen him – he was strutting along doing his cocky hard-man act with his board under his arm. The trouble is Magenta's so sweet and so trusting. And he looked as though he was really pestering her but Magenta's far too nice to say anything horrible to him. I just hoped I could catch up with them and intervene to protect her. That would certainly be spontaneous and manly with more than a hint of the oomph factor, I think. Oh Magenta! She was smiling politely at him and she looked so pretty. Then suddenly I felt my blood boil as I remembered how impressionable she'd been over the whole Adam Jordan business last year. I knew it was crucial that I spoke to her before she fell into the same trap with Ryan.

But, disaster! Before I could catch up with them, they turned into the staff car park. The last I saw of Magenta she was going through the main entrance while Ryan jumped on to his board and ollied down the railings of the steps into the quadrangle. That guy is such a show-off. But at least they weren't together, which was a huge relief. I was about to follow

Magenta when the bell went for registration. What a bummer! That meant that I wouldn't be able to see her again till break.

And then when I did – shock horror!

'Oh no!' Spud was pushing crisps into his mouth like there was a potato famine. I'd been trying to avoid looking at him because it was a bit like watching a concrete mixer. 'When did that happen?'

'What?' I said, picking half-chewed fragments of crisp off my jumper.

I was sitting on a wall in the upper school quadrangle with one eye on the door of the Humanities block, waiting to catch Magenta as she came out. Spud was staring over my shoulder. 'When did Magenta start going out with him?'

I turned round and nearly fell backwards into the litter-bin. I couldn't believe what I was seeing. I felt as though I'd been hit between the eyes by a Corellian Star Freighter. There, at the other side of the quad, was Magenta in full-on tongue tennis with the skateboard kid himself – Ryan Dunn! How could this have happened? I'd heard Curtis saying how cut up she was about us splitting up but here she was, less than a week after the break-up, snogging the tonsils off the King of Crud.

'Wazzup!' It was Magnus's moron brother, Angus.

'Daniel's in mourning, cos Ryan Dunn's on a Magenta-bender.'

'Shut up, Spud!' I could've decked him one. Like he wasn't upset as well!

'So what's the problem?'

'Shut up, Angus!' Anyone who had two brain cells to rub together knew what the problem was.

'You fancy her, right?' I sometimes think that, on the evolutionary scale, Angus has webbed feet. 'So I've got an idea.' Great, this was all I needed. Angus' last idea had resulted in the whole school standing on the playing field for two hours while three fire engines and a dozen firemen put a damper on his theory that the smoke detectors in the toilets were only there as a deterrent and didn't really work. That, coupled with his causing actual bodily harm to Anju's plait last week, and I was willing to bet that Angus' idea centred on pyromania of some description. I just hoped he wasn't going to suggest burning Magenta at the stake. 'You need to get her jealous.'

'Brilliant!' Spud agreed. I was beginning to think seriously about changing my circle of friends. 'How about Hattie?'

'What, Hattie Pringle?' I mean, Hattie's all right and everything but she's not a patch on Magenta.

'Yeah! She hasn't been out with anyone since she dumped Max May before Christmas, so the chances are she'll be gagging by now.' Spud has such a way with words.

'And you know what they say about Pringles . . .' I couldn't wait for Angus' contribution, '. . . once you pop you can't stop!'

'What's going on?' It was Magnus, the brother who'd inherited the brain cell – thank heavens for a bit of sanity.

'Nothing.' I glared at Spud, daring him to say any different.

'So what's my retard of a brother doing?'

I followed the line of Magnus' eyes. Eeek! Angus was talking to Hattie Pringle. And what was more, they were looking over in my direction and she was smiling and nodding. I felt sick.

'OK, so that's all set then,' Angus said when he came back. 'You're meeting her tomorrow night at seven o'clock in The Filling Station.' He offered me a high five but I felt more like punching his lights out. 'I did try to make it for tonight but she's got the auditions for the play – sorry mate.'

In the space of twelve hours I'd gone from being down in the pits to scaling the heights of anticipation – and suddenly I was plummeted down into the pits again. And not only that but, for the second time in five months, I've found myself going out with someone I don't really fancy while the girl of my dreams is off tickling tongues with every in-bred baboon in the neighbourhood. All this is doing my head in. From now on I'm just going to throw myself into my work with the stage crew and not even think about girls.

Alternatively – I could always brush up my strong and macho side.

5
Arlette

Phew! We managed to get out of that one. Actually, it's all thanks to Ms Lovell; she sorted it out. She and Magenta's dad took me home so that I didn't have to explain to Mum and Dad what had happened by myself. Ms Lovell is so nice. I don't know why Magenta moans about the fact that her dad's going out with her – I think she's fantastic.

My mum was furious at first. 'Have you taken leave of your senses, Arlette?' I learned a long time ago that with my parents (and with most adults, actually – in fact, with anybody of any age, come to think of it), silence is the best defence. So I didn't say anything. Although, I must be honest, I was a bit disappointed. I thought it would've been nice if either of them had said how relieved they were that they still had a daughter and that I hadn't gone up in a puff of smoke. 'What got into you? No one in their right mind tries to throw a pot on an electric drill!'

'You're forgetting, Gloria, *that girl* isn't in her right mind!' You know, for someone who prides himself on his religion and his holiness, my dad can be incredibly unforgiving sometimes. When he said that, I just wanted to curl up with embarrassment. I thought Magenta's dad took it remarkably well, though – in the circumstances.

I was just pleased that Ms Lovell was there. 'Now, Mr Jackson, I can see that you're angry but I think it might help the situation if we could all remember that Magenta is going through a difficult patch at the moment.'

She's just so calm about everything. Can you imagine how any normal adult would react if they came home to find mud hanging in stalactites from the ceiling, a record player that's been blown to pieces and their partner's daughter and her friend looking like escapees from Glastonbury? It's not exactly the scenario to induce love and understanding in most of the older generation, is it? I mean, I was petrified about going home and trying to explain to my mum and dad. But Magenta's dad and Ms Lovell were amazing.

'Magenta!' They looked a bit shocked when they first walked into the kitchen and then Ms Lovell just turned to Magenta's dad and said, 'It's all right, Curtis, I think I know what this is about.'

I will admit, he was looking a bit on the apoplectic side to start with. 'I don't care what it's about! What

I want to know is, what the hell's going on? I mean, how . . .? Who . . .?' To be honest, I think if Ms Lovell hadn't been there Madge and I might both have been in solitary confinement for the remaining duration of our natural lives.

'Girls, why don't you go upstairs and get washed. And Magenta, will you lend Arlette some clothes? Curtis, you take Sirius outside and hose him down while I start in here. We'll talk about what's happened when you're clean and tidy.'

I was starting to get really scared about what Mum and Dad were going to say and I was so mad I could hardly speak to Magenta. But it was amazing – by the time Ms Lovell had finished talking to all the parents you'd think we'd just saved the world or something. I thought at the very least I'd be banned from going to the auditions (or, if I'm being honest, I hoped I might be). But no such luck!

In fact, thanks to Ms Lovell, I've got Mum and Dad's blessing! 'You know, I think this school play will give the girls a healthy focus. It'll be something constructive to channel their energies into.'

Typical, isn't it? Having got one set of anxieties out of the way, there was another set to cope with: The auditions – and I don't mind telling you, I got myself into a bit of a state about the whole thing. My one and only experience of being on stage was a disaster that left me exhibiting my bright red underwear to the entire congregations of four churches! I was a laughing stock for months and the Popplewell boys called me 'Scarlet Arlette' until they emigrated to the Falkland Islands two years ago. I don't think I could stand it if anything like that happened again.

I cannot tell you how wound up I was all day at school.

'Hey, come on.' Ben did his best to cheer me up at break. 'How about if I come along too? We can do a duet together!' He started to prat about, holding my hand and pretending to do this sort of love song, which made me feel a little bit better.

We've been going out for six weeks now. I mean, he's really sweet and quite funny but I can't help comparing him to Daniel. I know Magenta's my best friend and everything but I seriously doubt her taste in boys. I mean, Daniel is way the nicest boy in the entire school and she dumped him because of some mystery sixth former he's supposed to be going out with. I mean, come on – that's about as likely as that Grade A bore in Year 12 asking *her* out. And speaking of Darien Quinn – you should've seen him at the auditions! He was wearing leather trousers that were so tight he looked as though he'd been vacuum-packed. And he'd gelled his hair into this enormous quiff – it was so big I'm surprised he didn't get whiplash when he turned his head. I don't know what gets into Magenta sometimes. It's like her internal radar homes in on every available loser. She's even agreed to go out with that deadhead Ryan Dunn, and he was horrible to her when she asked him to come to the auditions too.

'Sod off! Why would anyone want to be in a poncey play?'

She didn't seem that bothered though. 'Oh, it's going to be so exciting. I can hardly wait. I wonder what parts we'll get?'

Knowing Madge, she was probably counting on Ryan not being there so that she could suck up to Darien. And you wait, she'll probably get some major role and he'll go and fall for her and she'll come up smelling of roses. And Seema – well, what can I say about Seema? She'll probably be asked to produce it, or take it to the West End or something. She's brilliant at everything: I sometimes think that when God was giving out talent, Seema went round five times!

Anyway, I did manage to get through the whole of today without actually chucking up (which I think was verging on the miraculous), and when we got to the hall, it was quite a relief because there were only about thirty people there. There were only four of us from Year 9 – Magenta, me, Seema, and Hattie Pringle. She's quite cool.

'Hi, Hattie, I didn't know you were auditioning,' Seema said.

'It was Ms Keyes' idea really,' Hattie said. 'I'm taking Music next year with the voice as my instrument so she thought it might be good practice.' All these talented people. A teacher's never suggested I do anything.

The rest of them were mostly from Years 10 and 11 – with a few sixth-formers and a boy in Year 7 who does the porridge advert on television. I was glad Ben had come. Seema had talked Hayden into coming along too, so it didn't seem quite so scary. We were sitting near the front and Mr Grimsby was on the stage. He had a clipboard and was strutting about the place like one of those fat little Kelly dolls that my Auntie Gaynor's budgie bats around its cage.

'Right, now, I want the following to go with Ms Keyes into the music room.' Then he read out a list of names, including Magenta's. I know it probably sounds silly, because *Grease* is a musical, but it hadn't occurred to me that we'd have to have singing auditions. And, actually, I was quite pleased because

I'm in the choir at church, so I thought that I'd probably be OK in that section. 'Off you go, then,' Mr Grimsby shouted. 'Now, the next lot'll be going to the Drama studio with Miss Bignell for the dance auditions.' Aaggh! That hadn't occurred to me either and I suddenly started to feel queasy again. This time he read out my name and Seema's. Thank goodness we'd be together for moral support. I felt a bit sorry for Magenta being on her own. 'And those of you that're left, stay here for a read through.' That was Ben and Hayden's group. 'Then in about half an hour we'll swap groups. There's not many of you this year and we're running a bit later than we normally do, so I want to get this over with tonight. Come on then, jump to it.'

'Oooo! I'm in the same group as Darien,' Magenta said as she shot off towards the Music room. 'How lucky is that? I have such a good feeling about this audition.'

As our group went out towards the Drama studio I noticed Hattie looking up towards the lighting box and then she waved and blew a kiss. I knew she hadn't been out with anyone since before Christmas so I thought it would be really cool if I got all the goss before Magenta.

'Oh – who was that to?' I asked, casually.

'Daniel Davis,' she said, as though she hadn't just stabbed me in the back with a twelve-inch kitchen knife. 'He asked me out at break this morning.'

'I didn't know . . . How . . .? Erm . . .' I managed to compose myself. 'That's great, Hattie, but what's he doing up there?'

'He's in the stage crew. He didn't have to be here tonight but he's going to walk me home afterwards.' Hattie knew how upset I'd been when Daniel finished with me last year – in fact the whole year group knew how upset I'd been. And it was one thing for Magenta to go out with him because, after all, she does live next door to him and has had a sort of claim on him since they were both three. But Hattie! She was a complete outsider! And then she twisted the blade. 'And he's taking me to The Filling Station tomorrow after school. Isn't that sweet?'

The Filling Station had been our place. It was where Daniel had taken me. This was all I needed. Magenta may have had a good feeling about this audition but I just wanted to go home right there and then.

So the fact that the dancing went OK was pretty amazing really – considering the state I'd got myself into. Ms Bignell gave us this really simple routine to do that even a centipede with a hundred left feet could've managed. Seema's been going to tap and ballet since she was three so, naturally, she was the star of the show. But I think I did all right too. The next section was the singing – which I also thought went OK. I mean, I wasn't a patch on Seema or Hattie and there was this girl in Year 12 who sounded like she'd just stepped off the stage at the Opera House. But all in all I was quite pleased with myself.

After that I went back to the hall ready for our last audition, which was the reading. Magenta's group was still in there and Madge was on stage with Mr Marlowe, the other Drama teacher. She'd told me that she was going to get into costume for tonight but I hadn't quite been prepared for what I saw. Poor Madge. I think she must've had some sort of problem with her outfit because it looked like Mr Marlowe was standing opposite one of the Tweenies.

Mr Grimsby was pacing up and down on the floor banging his head with his clipboard. 'You're supposed to be a sweet, vulnerable, naïve teenager – not Anne Robinson in pigtails and bobby socks!' I hoped there was a trained first-aider on hand; I've never seen anyone who was about to have a heart attack but I think Mr Grimsby was probably pretty close.

'But, Sir, that's not realistic,' Magenta had her

hands open like she was appealing to the ref.

Mr Grimsby looked up at the ceiling and shook his head. 'A performance like that and she talks about realism!' Then he turned back to the stage. 'Well, thanks, Magenta – you certainly are the weakest link. Goodbye.'

'But, Sir. . .' I felt so sorry for her. Just then Ms Lovell went up to Mr Grimsby and whispered something to him.

'All right, then. One last go. And I mean it – this is your very last chance.'

Magenta read her part again and I have to say, she did come across as a bit on the domineering side but then, I suppose any role is open to interpretation, isn't it?

Mr Grimsby tossed his clipboard down in this weary sort of way. 'Right then you lot – off you go to the Drama studio. Next group, let's be having you.'

As Magenta went out she waved to Seema and me. 'This is so brilliant. I think the Grim Reaper likes me at last. I'm so pleased I managed to watch the video last night and really got into the part.' She flicked her bunches. I couldn't help wondering how she'd managed to find the time to watch a video after all that pot throwing and clearing up and everything. I was whacked by the time I went to bed. 'I think it really paid off, you know, because he asked to hear me five times! Can you believe it? And you should've heard Darien – he is *so* fantastic! He knocks spots off John Travolta. Bye – see you later.'

Mr Grimsby was handing out scripts. All the girls were reading one of Sandy's scenes while Mr Marlowe read in for Danny. Then the boys were reading a different Danny part while Ms Lovell read in for Sandy. I thought it'd gone quite well – no one had trodden on me or de-robed me, which had to be an improvement on my last venture into the acting world. But then, right at the end, Mr Grimsby and Mr Marlowe sat with their heads together for ages. People from the other groups were starting to come back in and Mr Grimsby stood up.

'OK, I'd like to hear Arlette Jackson again.' Me! I felt as sick as a parrot. I know he'd asked Magenta to read five times (which she seemed to think was a good thing), but I'd got the distinct impression that it was because she'd fluffed it. 'Chris,' he said to Mr Marlowe, 'have you got that scene with Sandy and Frenchy?' Mr Marlowe handed him the script. 'Champion! Right. Belinda, will you do the honours and read Sandy for us and Arlette, will you read Frenchy?'

My knees were like a pair of gyrating jellies and my throat started to seize up. I don't know how I got through it but I did.

It was nearly half-past six by the time it all finished and everyone was back in the hall. Ben came and sat with his arm round me and Seema and Hayden were getting all cosy on the row behind us. Hattie was sitting in the row in front but she was facing the back of the hall, obviously so she could see Daniel. I couldn't believe how miffed I was about her and Daniel. I mean, I do like Ben and everything – and I was pleased that I was going out with someone. I mean, I didn't want Daniel to think that I was a pathetic loser who couldn't get a boyfriend but (and I'm not very proud of this), there is another part of me that wants him to know I still like him. I mean, if Daniel asked me out again, I'd dump Ben like a shot. And I know you probably think that's a horrible thing to say but it's true. So, I was sort of sitting half with my back to Ben, just in case Daniel should look down and think that I wasn't still an option.

I felt a bit sorry for Magenta, actually – she was the only one of our little group not to have her boyfriend there.

'How did it go?' I asked her.

'Honestly! That stupid Bignell woman!'

'What, the dancing?' I couldn't think what could possibly have gone wrong; the routine had been so simple.

'Well, you know the bit where we had to go step, step, step, kick to the right and then step, step, step, kick to the left?' I nodded. 'OK, well we'd done the bit to the right, right? And then I looked down and my shoe lace was undone.' Uh oh. I hoped Magenta wasn't going to say what I thought she was going to say. 'Well, what was I supposed to do? Carry on until I tripped up and broke my leg?'

'So what happened?'

'I did what any normal person would do – I bent down to tie it.'

Just then this sixth former walked past rubbing her arm. She looked as though she'd been crying. 'Moron!' she spat as she went by.

Then a couple of Year 11 boys came in and handed Mr Grimsby an A4 pad. One of them was limping. 'Sorry we're late, Sir. We've been with Michael Kelly and Ms Bignell in the medical room. His nose is bleeding so Ms Bignell said to carry on without them, but these are her notes.'

Magenta seemed put out. 'Honestly! They didn't take *me* to the medical room. And it's not pleasant having half-a-dozen of the upper school land on top of you, you know. I think I might even have bruised a rib.'

'Right, listen up everybody.' Mr Grimsby was on the stage now. 'Most of you we know from your lessons or previous productions but there's a few newcomers and some hidden talent out there and I think I'm speaking for all the staff here today when I say that . . .' he paused and watched Ms Bignell as she came in and sat down with Michael Kelly. He was covered with blood and was holding a humungous wodge of cotton wool to his face.

'He was the one who started it,' Magenta whispered. 'He didn't look where he was going, he just went smack, right into me when I was bending down to tie my lace. It's lucky he skidded a bit or else he would've got blood all over my blouse.'

Mr Grimsby gave a little cough, '. . . when I say that, almost without exception . . .' I'm sure he looked over in our direction when he said that. '. . . the standard's been even better than ever this year. We're looking for half-a-dozen soloists and then another dozen or so to be in the chorus and to take on some of the smaller roles.'

'Ooo! I can hardly wait.' Magenta squeezed my arm. Then she seemed to notice Hattie smiling up at the lighting box for the first time. 'Who's she looking at?'

Eeesh! I hadn't really wanted to be the one to tell her. 'Er, Daniel.' I thought if I said it quickly, it might, sort of, slip by unnoticed.

'Daniel? What, *my* Daniel?' She looked up at the box. 'It *is* my Daniel! What's he doing up there?'

'Apparently he's in the stage crew.'

'What, Daniel? Since when? How long have you known about this, Arl?' Oops! 'And what's going on with him and Hattie?'

'He's not *your* Daniel, Madge. You finished with him – remember?'

She looked a bit peed off at that.

'Girls! I'm waiting.' Mr Grimsby did not look a happy man. 'Right. In the role of Danny, we've got Darien Quinn.'

Magenta gripped my arm in excitement, suddenly distracted from Daniel. 'Oh, he will be sooooo fantastic. You should see the way he moves.'

'. . . and as Sandy, we've chosen a newcomer . . .'

I thought Magenta was going to explode. 'I knew there was a reason he wanted me to read it five times!'

'. . . Seema Karia. Well done, Seema.'

Wow! How amazing is that? Didn't I say Seema

was good at everything? I turned round and gave her a big hug.

Seema was quite overcome. 'I can't believe it!'

Hayden gave her a big squishy kiss on the head. 'Well done, hon!'

'Yes – excellent, Seema.' I thought Magenta didn't sound quite as pleased as the rest of us, but maybe she was just thinking about Daniel and Hattie and that stuff.

'In the role of Kenickie, Hayden West . . .' this was amazing – both Seema and her boyfriend had main parts. There was a Year 11 girl as Rizzo but then, wait for this, '. . . and as Frenchy, Arlette Jackson.'

I was so blown away. I could hardly believe it. Seema and I hugged each other and then hugged Ben and Hayden. How brilliant was that? But Mr Grimsby was reading out a list of the chorus now and Ben's name was there and so was Hattie's. Then he folded up his sheet of paper and looked round the hall.

'Congratulations to those of you who've been successful. Rehearsal times will be posted on the notice board – you do not miss a rehearsal unless you're in intensive care or there's an imminent earthquake – understood?' We all nodded. 'For those of you who didn't get picked this time, don't give up. You can always come along and support Ms Lovell who'll be doing set design and props – and of course, there's always next year. Well done, everybody.'

We were all so excited and bouncing about on our seats that we didn't really notice that Magenta hadn't got a part.

'He's forgotten to read out my name. I can't believe he'd do that. How could this've happened?' She was looking a bit shell-shocked.

'Oh, Madge, I'm sure it's just a mistake. Go and ask him,' I said.

But Ms Lovell had already got there. She was on the stage talking to Mr Grimsby and they were looking in Magenta's direction. Mr Grimsby was shaking his head but then he gave a big sigh and shouted, 'OK, and the chorus'll have Magenta too.'

'See, it was just an oversight,' I said, trying to make her feel better.

'Yeah! Right!' She pulled the elastics out of her hair as she walked off and tossed them into the bin. 'That man hates me!'

'Leave her,' Seema said, taking my arm and stopping me from going after her. 'I think the last thing she wants is for either of us to be with her right now. Let's give her some space – you know how much this meant to her.' She was right, of course.

Just then, there was this terrible noise echoing round the empty corridors. It sounded like a giant in seven league boots was thumping down the stairs but when we looked round, it was Daniel leaping down the staircase from the lighting box. He shot past us, skidded along the wooden floor, into the litterbin, did a sort of judo-style sideways roll, leapt up and carried on running. Wow! It was really athletic the way he did that.

'Hey, Daniel! Wait!' Hattie called out.

He turned round so that he was running backwards. 'Hi, Hattie! Can't stop. See you tomorrow!' The trouble was, as he turned round again, he went wallop, straight into one of the display boards in the entrance hall that had the mock GCSE Art projects on them. Daniel spread-eagled against it, trying to stop it falling over; teetered for a split second, then both he and the display board fell over with a deafening crash. Everyone who was still in the hall came running out to see what had happened and Hattie and I both dashed over to help him.

'Are you OK?' Hattie said, bending down. You'd have thought she would've actually done something to help him, wouldn't you? I mean, she is supposed to be his girlfriend!

At least I helped him to his feet and offered him a comforting arm round his shoulder. 'You're not hurt, are you?'

'No, no – I'm fine.'

'What happened?' Ms Lovell was next on the scene.

Poor Daniel looked a bit embarrassed. 'I was in a bit of a rush to see if Ma ...' he stopped, mid sentence, '... Ma ... my ... my dinner was ready. Yes, that's it – I was rushing home to get my dinner and I tripped. Sorry.'

'No harm done,' Ms Lovell said. 'Oh – or at least, not *much* harm done.'

Oops! When we'd picked up the display board all the artwork was intact except for one piece.

'Typical!' Daniel said. 'I might as well sign my death warrant now!'

The painting was in the category 'Games and Pastimes'. The main part was a fairly ordinary painting of a Super Mario kart but then the bonnet came out as a three dimensional, papier-mâché Transformer-type arm with a pipe-cleaner figure in its clutches. I'd seen it earlier in the week and thought how menacing it looked. The trouble was it now looked about as menacing as a floppy concertina.

I rubbed Daniel's arm to make him feel better. 'I'm

sure your brother'll understand if you explain it was an accident.' But he looked at me as though I'd just landed from another planet.

Ben took my hand and led me away, 'Hey, come on, Frenchy, I'll walk you to the bus stop. Later, Danno!'

For a minute I'd forgotten about the play and getting such a big part. I couldn't wait to phone my sister Cassie at university and tell her. I was so excited! I'm so pleased Magenta talked me into doing the audition. I just hope she'll be OK.

6
Magenta

The first day of the half-term holidays and am I looking forward to it? I don't think so!

I can't believe my dad has done this to me. He's subjecting me to seven days (and nights!) of mental, emotional and fashion torture from my dork of a cousin. Can you believe it? Honestly, it's bad enough that we go there most Christmases and I have to sleep in Justine's room. She's all, 'Let's do each other's hair, Magenta.' And 'Let's paint each other's nails, Magenta.' And 'I wish we were sisters, Magenta.' She drives me nuts. I thought I'd got out of it this year because their family went skiing at Christmas, so we could stay at home (hallelujah!) but now, just because my dad wants his brother here to help him prepare for the party, I'm going to have to share my bedroom with her for practically the entire week. Parents can be so selfish sometimes. I mean, wouldn't you have thought that, as the caring parent he tries to make out he is, he would've appreciated what a hard time I've been having recently and given me a break?

I mean, take the auditions, for example. He gave me no support whatsoever.

'Maybe drama's not your thing, love. You can't be good at everything.' Which is so not true, because Seema is.

'It's that stupid Grimsby man – he hates me. I could be the next Gwyneth Paltrow and he wouldn't've given me a part – on principle!' And that *is* true. I wouldn't mind but I did exactly what the Grim Reaper had said I should – I really got into the part. I put my hair in bunches and I wore my PE shoes and white ankle socks. I even borrowed Gran's nylon sticky-out petticoat thing that she used to wear when she first started going out with Grandad. But did he give me one gramme of credit? No way!

Oh, it was so humiliating I just wanted to die. He slipped me in at the end like an afterthought; 'Oh and we'll have Magenta too.' He might as well have added, 'If we really have to.' I still think it was that mollusc-featured Mr Marlowe's fault with his stupid goatee beard. I mean, how was I supposed to act opposite him when he looks as though he's got a slug crawling down his chin? Distracting, or what? And anyway, if he hadn't read Danny in such a wimpy way then my Sandy wouldn't have come over as being so bossy. It doesn't require a psychologist to work that out, now does it?

And everything had been going so brilliantly till then – well, maybe not brilliantly, but quite well anyway. Belinda and I had had a good, long chat about everything and she'd agreed to let me off the pottery assignment and also not to switch me into Mrs Joshua's group. And Arlette and I had got all our stuff sorted out. It turns out her parents had got completely the wrong idea about me. You see, Arlette's mum is a history teacher who knows old Jones the Bones and he'd been filling her head with all sorts of lies. Honestly! I wonder if I've got a case against him for defamation? But, anyway, Arlette and I are friends again now – not that I ever doubted we would be. We're too mature to allow silly squabbles to get between us.

And the other brilliant thing that happened was that Ryan Dunn asked me out. I mean, how fantastic is that? (Or at least I thought it was fantastic at the time – I'll be honest, I'm not so sure at the moment. It's all going a bit pear-shaped, but I'll tell you about that later.) Anyway, to go back to last week; it was the morning after the unfortunate pottery accident and the day of the awful unmentionables (the auditions). I was just on my way into school when I heard this, 'Chung-chung, chung-chung,' coming down the road. And then Ryan suddenly zoomed around in front of me on his skateboard.

'Hi!' He sort of flicked his board up and caught it in one hand. Oooo! I thought, how professional is that? Then he walked along next to me with his board under his arm. At one point he gave this cheeky little wave to Mr Onanije who was on gate-duty – you should've seen Mr Onanije's face. Anyway, I started to tell Ryan how seeing him in Technology had given me this brilliant idea for throwing a pot, when he suddenly butted in. 'So, do you fancy going out with me, then?'

Wow! It was only twenty to nine in the morning so I thought there was a chance I might be still suffering the remnants of sleep-induced deafness. 'Me?'

'Well, I'm not in the habit of talking to the wall.'

Ooo! Talk about firm and to the point. 'OK,' I said, trying to sound really cool. Actually, I could hardly believe it. I mean, I know he'd smiled at me – but to ask me out!

'Cool! See you in the quad at break then,' he said. Then, as soon as we were out of sight of Mr Onanije, he jumped on to his board again, skated down the drive into the staff car park and seemed to just bounce up on to the handrail of the little steps leading down into the quad. Wow! I was so impressed – not just with his skating but the fact that he doesn't let silly school rules bother him. And the other thing that I really like about him is, even when he's in school uniform he manages to look really cool. All the other boys wear these gross, regulation nylony-type trousers but Ryan has these grey phat pants that look brilliant. He manages to get away with wearing trainers as well. The only time I tried that I ended up having to have my feet inspected twice a day for a fortnight by Miss Crumm, the head of PE – not an experience I want to repeat in a hurry. She pulled my toes apart till I thought they were going to snap off, saying she was looking for evidence of fungal infections – ugh! Gross!

Anyway, I was telling Arlette and Seema about Ryan in registration. Mr Kingston was discussing the footie with some of the boys and Candy Meekin, so we were talking about friends and relationships and stuff like that.

'And he just came straight out with it – "Do you fancy going out with me, then?" Just like that. He didn't get his mates to ask me, or anything.'

'That's because he hasn't got any mates,' Arlette said. (I think she was a teensy bit nervous about the auditions that night.)

'Yes he has. He's got lots of friends.'

'Only Perry Proctor and the Portakabin posse,' she said, referring to the boys from the behavioural unit.

'That's so not true!' We'd only just made up after the night before so I didn't want to be too down on her.

'Well, you have to admit, Madge, yesterday you said you really liked that sixth former and last week you said you really liked Daniel.'

Honestly! There I was making allowances for her because she was nervous and suddenly she's on my case like the Amazing Memory Woman. 'When I said I liked Daniel, I meant I liked him as a friend – that's all.' Had I really said I liked him? What a deluded idiot I must've been! 'But anyway, that was before I knew what he was really like. And as for Darien, I said I liked him, I didn't say I wanted to marry him. But, it won't do my reputation any harm to have a boyfriend, will it?'

Actually, when she'd said that it was a bit of a shocker. I'd been so excited about Ryan asking me out that I'd temporarily forgotten about Darien and, after all, he was the whole reason for going to the auditions in the first place. And, boy, was he worth it! I mean, the rest of the evening was a total write-off but Darien had to be seen to be believed. I mean, I really don't want to dwell on the whole auditions thing but you should've seen him – he was wearing these leather trousers and he'd slicked back his hair. Ronan Keating, eat your heart out! And he kept smiling at me in this really nice way – you know, like you do when you think someone's cute and funny. And he even spoke to me a few times. He's got this great sense of humour – subtle but witty. But I guess that comes with maturity.

For example, in the singing part of the audition, Ms Keyes kept pointing her finger and saying, 'You, the Year 7 girl on the front row – keep quiet. The rest of you let's take it from the top.'

I hadn't a clue who she was talking to until Darien leaned forward and whispered, 'She means you.'

'But I'm not Year 7. I'm Year 9.'

'Yes, but I think she's going on appearances.' See? It was an obvious reference to all the effort I'd made on my costume – what a tease!

But anyway, as I said, I don't want to talk about the auditions. As far as I'm concerned it's over and done with. I've put the whole sorry episode behind me and moved on. But, when I was waiting for my turn to read, I couldn't help overhearing Darien talking to a group of Year 11 boys.

'Well, it's in my blood. When my mother was at the Palladium she was working with Sir John

Mills one time and he said to her, "Patsy . . ." '

I didn't get a chance to hear the end of the story because I was called up on to the stage, but how amazing is that? Darien's mother was on stage with someone who's a Sir – and not just in the teachery way of calling someone 'sir' either. Honestly, I don't think I've ever met anyone who had so many things going for them – his looks, his clothes, his acting – even his mother is a plus. Now, how often can you say *that* about someone? And he was really sweet to me after that stupid Year 11 boy tripped up and kicked me in the ribs.

He said, 'Next year we'll have to do *Calamity Jane* and you can play the lead.' Now when someone like Darien recognises that I have the ability to play a lead, it really means something to me because he knows what he's talking about. I bet that stupid Grimsby man hasn't got a drop of actors' blood in a single one of his veins.

But anyway, as I keep saying, I don't want to talk about the auditions – although, another little shocker was to find out that Daniel's somehow got himself into the stage crew. Don't ask me how because it's not usually open to anyone under Year 10. It's probably his older woman who's wangled it for him. Actually, if I'm being totally honest, I am still a bit annoyed with him. I mean, he'd not only two-timed me with that sixth former but now he's going out with Hattie Pringle – which means that either:

a) he's getting through girlfriends like most people get through bags of crisps or,

b) he's now two-timing the sixth former.

And, if you follow the whole 'leopard and spots' theory of human behaviour, it's probably the latter. I mean, so much for saying how upset he was about us finishing! But, if Daniel wants to follow the Davis family tradition, that's none of my business. And anyway, at least now that we're both going out with other people (plural in his case), we're sort of talking again. Which brings me to yesterday.

You see I had this brilliant idea. Now, contact me @greatexpectations.com but I thought that when a boy and girl were 'going out', they actually went out. Silly me! It seems that Ryan's list of exciting places to take his girlfriend (i.e. me) extends from the bus terminus, to the ramps underneath the motorway. Not only that, but any sort of romance I might have dreamed of also has to include Perry Proctor and his posse, the Leonardo lot (Ryan's gang from his old school), and several dozen skateboards! Not *exactly* what I'd had in mind when he first asked me out.

But never let it be said that I'm not flexible. I mean, if Ryan doesn't want to go out on a date that doesn't involve a skateboard, then I decided I'd have to take the date to Ryan. It was quite simple – I'd have to learn to board.

Teensy bit of a problem though, because I've been a bit phobic about anything with wheels ever since an unfortunate incident with Gran's roller train when I was about six. You see, when Mary next-door went back to work, Gran used to childmind Daniel and Joe after school. It was great until one day she turned up in the playground with this carrier bag full of a job lot of roller-skates that she'd bought from the charity shop. We all sat there in the playground while she put these skates on us. Then it was like she was doing the Indian rope trick because she pulled out a mahoosive length of washing line too and told us we all had to hang on to it. Even as I'm telling you, I can feel myself going cold. I mean, it doesn't take the Minister of Transport to imagine the potentially lethal consequences, now does it? Anyway, Gran went on the front of the roller train (she told us she was the engine) and Joe went on the back – he'd got a pair of Fisher-Price roller-blades for his birthday, so he was slightly less wobbly than Daniel and me.

'All aboard! Choo, choo!' she shouted.

I can remember feeling really excited – for about half a millisecond! And then it was like, scary-ville all the way home – especially when we got to the top of our road, which just happens to be on a slight incline. I mean, we're not talking Mount Everest or anything but definitely steep enough to have built up a fair amount of momentum by the time Mrs Pickles' cat, Geranium, ran out. The human pile-up was not a pretty sight. The only one who didn't end up on the heap was Joe. He'd let go of the rope and I remember seeing him zooming past us with his arms windmilling backwards. Thankfully he couldn't quite negotiate the bend so he didn't end up squashed on the main road. Instead he nose-dived into old Mr Wurzell's topiary hedge.

Mary sent the boys to Terry Prendergast's mum after that and poor old Mr Wurzell ended up in a home – shame, I used to like his garden.

Anyway, my relationship with anything to do with wheels has been somewhat tainted as a result, so I just hoped Ryan appreciated the effort I was putting into going out with him. I didn't have enough money to buy a proper skateboard so I'd decided to employ my creative genius and build one. That's what's so nice about being artistic – nothing's impossible.

Anyway, I'd rummaged about and found the bag of skates that Gran had bought all that time ago and I commandeered an old tray from the kitchen. I mean when you think about it, that's all a skateboard is, isn't it? A tray with wheels at each end. The only difference was, mine had the wheels taped on with about a thousand layers of sticky tape. Admittedly, it wasn't ideal and the sticky tape wasn't quite as secure as rivets but I thought it would get me used to the whole rolling thing after all these years. It was just then that Daniel looked over the fence. (The bruise round his eye had gone through the whole rainbow since last week but it was down to a sort of faded yellowy colour now. Arlette told me that Joe hadn't been at all understanding when he found out about the damage to his artwork.)

'You'll break your leg if you're not careful.' I still wasn't speaking to him at that point, so I was a tad peed off. Like, who did he think he was? My father? 'I've got my old skateboard in the shed if you want to borrow it.'

Now, never let it be said that I'm proud. If Daniel wanted to offer the hand of friendship, then I was happy to accept it. And anyway, every time I put a foot on my tray creation, it tipped up sideways and I whacked myself in the calf.

'Thank you.' I just made sure that he knew there was a distinct difference between me graciously accepting his offer and actually forgiving him for how he'd behaved. But then when I saw what he produced, I wasn't too sure about the 'graciously accepting' bit either. What he hadn't made clear was how he defined the word *old*. You see I'd thought that 'old' meant 'not new'. Daniel, however, obviously thought it meant 'hideously out of date'. He handed me this grotesque thing that looked as though it'd been rejected by the dustmen. It was luminous green plastic with one of the Teenage Mutant Ninja Turtles on it, looking all scratched and battered.

'What is *that*?'

'Fine! Don't borrow it then.' He sounded a bit peed off. 'I know it's hardly the Porsche of the skating world but I think it's marginally up-market from your scrap-heap challenge.' He started to take the board back.

Then I felt a teensy bit guilty because I had a vague memory of Daniel's dad buying it for him when he was about eight. 'No,' I said, 'it's great – really!' I mean, it would be OK to use it for practising – it wasn't like anyone would see me.

He stood there for a while watching me which, I

have to admit was a bit embarrassing because every time I went to get on it, the stupid thing rolled away. I ended up scooting along the patio like a three year old doing fairy steps with one foot.

'It's OK now, Daniel – I can manage.' I wanted him to go – I was sure he was gloating.

'Do you know how to skate?' Gggrrr! Although, he did have a point. I hadn't realised there was a technique. I thought if I just stood on it, it would roll. Well, it did, but not in the way I wanted it to.

'Yes.' But just then the board shot out from under my foot, flipped up and crashed down on to the stone. 'Well, sort of.'

'Do you want me to teach you?'

What a dilemma! There was no way I wanted Daniel getting all smug and thinking I was going to let him off the hook for the way he treated me. Although, I did think Ryan would be really impressed if, when I turned up for our date, I could do a few things on a board – like, stay on it, for starters.

'Well, all right then,' I tried to make it sound as though I was doing him a big favour by letting him teach me.

'OK, let's go down the park. There's more space there.'

The park! I didn't want anyone I knew to see me with Daniel's scummy skateboard. 'What, with this?'

And then he seemed to go into Incredible Hulk mode. 'You know what, Magenta – forget it! Forget I even offered. Give it back and you just carry on with your *Blue Peter*-style tray on wheels.'

WoooOooo! So who'd been rattling his cage? Obviously the strain of having so many girlfriends was beginning to tell. But then I looked at what I had been using and it did look a teensy bit like one that Sirius had made earlier. 'I didn't mean it in *that* way . . .'

'What way *did* you mean it, then?' Goodness! Daniel can be surprisingly firm sometimes.

'I just meant that I didn't want you to risk taking your board to the park because I know it's precious to you and it might get lost or damaged.' Phew! I think I got away with it, and it wasn't a total lie – well, it was but I had my fingers crossed behind my back, so it didn't count. I'd just have to be careful that no one saw me.

'Take Sirius with you, will you, love?' Gran was on the phone to Auntie Vee as I left. 'And be careful. We don't want any broken ankles for the party, do we?'

Great! That was all I needed. My street cred was

going to be subterranean if I wasn't careful. Not only was I going to be with Daniel (whose latest haircut gave him more than a passing resemblance to Sonic the Hedgehog), but I was carrying a Day-Glo board with a cartoon turtle on it and now I'd got Sirius in tow, whose excitement levels have been known to evacuate entire beaches before now. Hardly inconspicuous! I just hoped that at ten-thirty on a Saturday morning, Ryan and his gang would still be asleep.

And actually the morning went surprisingly well. We stayed on the asphalt part between the tennis courts and the bowling green at the top end of the park because it's nice and flat up there.

There were signs everywhere saying:

'DOGS MUST BE KEPT ON A LEASH –
PENALTY £200'

so I had to tie Sirius' lead to the fence. The last thing I wanted was for him to be running around like a loony and barking at every bird, leaf or human that came within a fifty-yard radius so that Dad got fined. (I know you're probably thinking that Sirius is my dog, which strictly speaking he is – but where am I going to get two hundred pounds? Get real.) Anyway he was being very well-behaved and I was really enjoying myself – and, more to the point, I was getting the hang of it really quickly. And, actually, I hate to admit it but Daniel was amazingly good. Not up to Ryan's standard, obviously, but not at all bad.

I don't know how long we'd been there – probably a couple of hours – when Daniel seemed to go all serious on me. There I was, bombing along towards the public toilets at quite a speed (in fact Daniel was running alongside but he was having a job keeping up with me) when suddenly, he just blurted out, 'I was never going out with Samantha Campion, you know.'

Out of the blue, or what? 'Ooooh!' I wobbled perilously but Daniel reached out and managed to catch me. I hadn't quite mastered the stopping part yet. 'What did you just say?'

We'd been having such fun but suddenly Daniel looked as though he was about to break some really tragic news. 'I didn't cheat on you, you know, Magenta.'

Yeah! Right! But actually, he said it so seriously that if I hadn't seen him and that older woman with my own eyes, I might even have believed him. 'I don't want to talk about it. Anyway, it's ancient history now. I'm going out with Ryan and you're going out with Hattie, so let's just leave it at that.'

'But I'm not,' he said. 'I was talking to Mum . . .' Uh oh! Mary's very nice and everything, but she's a bit OTT on the self-help armchair-psychology books. '. . . and she pointed out that by going out with Hattie, I wasn't acting with integrity, so I finished with her last night.'

Integrity? Another new word to commit to memory so that I could look it up when I went home. 'Oh – that's good,' I said, trying to sound as though I knew what he was talking about. 'Well, anyway, I'm still going out with Ryan and I'm meeting him at four o'clock at the bus depot, so could we get on with the lesson now, please?'

'Look, let's go and get a cup of tea.'

I was getting the distinct impression that Daniel wanted the conversation to take on an Oprah-type intensity. 'It's OK. You go and get one if you want. I'll stay here and practise.'

I hadn't even been speaking to Daniel two hours ago and suddenly he wanted us to have a heart to heart? Giant leap, I think! Anyway he went off to the little café by the main gate and I stayed by the tennis courts but, to be honest, it was a bit boring on my own – just skateboarding backwards and forwards. And, actually, my legs were starting to ache. Not only that, but I was sure Sirius must be getting bored.

'Come on, boy,' I said to Sirius, 'let's go and find Daniel and go home.'

I had thought of skateboarding down to the café but it was on a slight gradient and horrific memories of Gran's roller train came flooding back but then I had a brainwave. If I sat on the skateboard, Sirius could pull me along and if he went too quickly or anything it would be easy to put my feet down to stop myself because I'd be sitting down. Brilliant! And it would be fun for him too after he'd been tied up for all that time. I had a quick look round to check that no one was looking (because I didn't think it was exactly cool to be seen sitting on a skateboard being pulled along by a dog), but the place was deserted – it was the middle of February after all.

'Giddy up!' I said, giving Sirius' lead a shake. This was amazing! I had to give poor little Sirius a bit of a push off but once we got rolling it was wicked. We were moving at a fairly unspectacular speed to begin with (thank goodness), although it did start to pick up a bit as we trundled down towards the café.

And then I saw her!

'Coo-ee! Magenta!' It was Janet Dibner and her brother John from Year 8. (Did I ever mention the fact that their parents run the local kennels? Well, they do.) And there, about a hundred yards in front of me, were Janet, John and nine dogs, ranging in size from a Great Dane to a Shih tzu, obviously having their daily constitutional. Uh oh! Now, Sirius is the friendliest, most confident animal in the world when he's with humans but introduce him to anything with four legs and he presses the rewind button faster than you can say 'Wily Coyote'. Before I knew what had happened, Sirius had wrenched his lead from my hand, done a hasty U-turn and headed back up towards the tennis courts – with eight out of the nine dogs hot on his tail. The only one left was a geriatric Old English Sheepdog who seemed to be dragging Janet back out of the gate as she screamed at John, 'Catch them!' It was like something out of a Winalot advert – dogs everywhere, all barking and bouncing about and I was unable to go to poor Sirius' aid, because I was still careering downhill in contra-flow of the canine stampede. I have to admit, I was beginning to panic until suddenly I saw my salvation.

'Move!' I screamed at Janet. The gateway to the park had one of those rails that's just high enough to let a pushchair underneath but too low for a bike, so I decided that my best bet of surviving this without the need for plastic surgery was to grab the rail as I went under it. The trouble was, Janet was standing

115

slap bang in the middle, heaving at the sheepdog to come back. Just when I thought I had no alternative but to jump off and risk serious internal and external injury, the dog seemed to have worked out that the fun was happening in the opposite direction so lurched free of his handler and began bounding up the path. Unfortunately, Daniel was just coming out of the café with two cups of tea when the lumbering animal (who, let's be fair, couldn't see a thing because of the mop of hair flopping all over his face – reminded me a bit of Spud, actually) went crashing into him. All I saw as I zoomed past was Daniel hurtling upwards and brown steamy liquid flying everywhere.

'Aaagggggh!'

But I couldn't do anything because I was going to require all my concentration to make this work.

'Mooooove!' I shouted again.

'YES! How about that! Ms Bignell would've been proud of me. I knew Year 7 gym club would pay off one day. As the skateboard went under the railing, Janet Dibner leapt sideways into the rose bed (luckily the roses had been pruned so she wasn't too badly scratched) and I reached up and grabbed the bar. Then, as the board rolled out from under me, I swung my legs forward, arching my back beautifully, before going into a perfect pike as I swung back. Tra-la! I stood up – totally unscathed. Sadly the same couldn't be said for Daniel's skateboard. There was a sickening crunch from somewhere out on the road and then the driver of an articulated lorry wound down his window and began hurling abuse at me. Honestly! Some people are so unreasonable. I don't think he realised that if it hadn't been for my gymnastic prowess, he could've found himself up on a manslaughter charge.

Anyway, it took the four of us almost an hour to round up all the dogs and then (despite a slight scald to his hand and a bruised elbow), Daniel thought the least we could do was help Janet and John back to the kennels with them. So, by the time I got home, it was much later than I'd realised. Of course, Dad went ballistic because I hadn't tidied my room what with the muppets arriving tomorrow and everything, so he banned me from going down to the bus depot to meet Ryan. Honestly! We've been going out ten days and we haven't actually *been out* yet. All we do is see each other at school – which is OK, but I've had so many boring rehearsals for this stupid play that even that's been limited. Anyway, I'm sure we'll find masses of time to meet up in the holidays – if I can get away from my cousin Justine, that is.

Whoa! Would somebody please explain how this has happened? The last time I saw my cousin Justine she was still in the Jurassic period as far as sophistication was concerned. So what's been going on? Has Uncle Wayne been slipping growth hormone into her orange juice, or has she been abducted by aliens and replaced by some android version that looks vaguely facially similar? This is unreal!

Their car pulled up, right? Out gets Auntie Heather – no change there. Then Uncle Wayne (he's great) – no change. Likewise with the munchkin, Holden – (unfortunately) no change there. But then there's this person sitting where Justine usually sits in the car – only her hair is all sticking up and punky – and it's got bright red streaks in it! And her ears are pierced – in three places! And – wait for it –

SHE'S ONLY TALKING ON A MOBILE PHONE!

Just wait till I speak to my dad about this. This is *so* not fair!

7
Daniel

'Daniel!' Magenta was calling my name from somewhere but I couldn't work out where. 'Daniel!' She shook my shoulders. She's so beautiful. I reached out my arms to pull her towards me. I felt so happy. I could feel myself smile with anticipation of her kiss. Oh Magenta!

'Ugh! Gerroff me!' Her voice sounded strangely high pitched as she pushed me away. Then a wet flannel smacked me in the face. 'Daniel, wake up!' I was eyeball to eyeball with Holden Orange, the brat from hell who seems to've been put on this earth for the sole purpose of bringing misery to thousands – and me in particular.

'What?' I was amazed at the amount of hostility I could project into one simple word.

It was five days since Holden had been inflicted on me – together with an enormous glass jar containing his colony of eighty-three stick insects (including babies). And, during that time, my caring sharing qualities have been tested to the limit. In fact, they'd probably gone beyond the limits of any self-respecting male.

I know this is nothing to be proud of but, in the beginning, I did think that I might be able to use his precociously evil genius to my advantage. You know, wreak all sorts of revenge on my brother. But when, by Wednesday, I found myself sentenced to a whole day of solitary confinement while the Gremlin was treated to a day at the Leisure Centre with Curtis and his dad, I realised that my little plan had hideously backfired.

Take last Monday for instance: he'd been in the house less than twenty-four hours and already I was in trouble. *Me* – not Holden!

'Daniel!' Mum was standing on the landing looking as though she'd been nursing down a coal mine. Oops! 'I know this wouldn't be your idea but did you know anything about it?' She was almost breathing fire.

Now, as you know, lying has never been my strong point, so I couldn't deny that I'd known Holden's repertoire of pranks was going to kick off with that old favourite, smudgy soap. However, my attempt at mitigating circumstances didn't go down too well either. 'I did tell him not to put it in the bathroom till after you'd gone to work.' Which, if the little moron had listened to me, would've ensured that Joe was the only person likely to be on the receiving end.

'You are fourteen years old, Daniel – old enough to know better. Holden is only eight. This is totally irresponsible of you.' You see what I mean? Why was it irresponsible of *me*?

Then on Tuesday there was the classic, a tumbler of water balanced on a ruler above Joe's bedroom door.

'Only put about a centimetre of water in the bottom, OK?' I warned. 'Don't go filling it up or there'll be water everywhere and Mum'll go mad. We only want to damp him down a little bit.' I mean I couldn't have been clearer than that, now could I? But what I hadn't bargained for was the little nerd not only filling the plastic beaker to the brim, but also using an entire jar of green food colouring and a generous dollop of flour so that it was a disgustingly gloopy mess. Add to that the unforeseen death-wish factor of Joe bringing his girlfriend Anthea Pritchard home for a bit of a snog, and I'm sure I don't have to spell it out. Although I have to confess, even though I knew I would probably die a slow and painful death at the hands of my mother's first-born, seeing Anthea Pritchard standing there with green slime clogging up her nylon braids and dripping down her false eyelashes was totally worth it. And my second black

121

eye in two weeks was giving me quite a reputation as a hard man. Shame about the twenty-four hour confinement to my room though.

But, if Holden was an even bigger pain in the bum than Magenta had led me to believe, his sister Justine was the total opposite. I mean, from the way Magenta had described her, I'd pictured someone straight out of Enid Blyton. I think the last time they'd been down to stay with Curtis and Florence, Holden had been in a pushchair (which, when you think about it, would be the safest place for him now), so I couldn't really remember much about them but I was well impressed with Justine.

'Hi, Daniel.' They all came round to mine on Sunday just after they'd arrived, Magenta, Justine and the Pest. I've got to be honest, I wasn't really paying attention to Justine, I was more concerned about Magenta because she seemed really quiet. 'Cool room,' Justine said. She was going round picking up and examining everything that wasn't screwed to the wall. 'What games've you got?'

'Oh, loads. Have a look through if you like.' I looked across at Magenta. She looked really sad and I couldn't make out what was going on with her. I knew we'd been through a bit of a rough patch but we'd had a really brilliant day the day before.

It had been the first day of half-term. I'd heard all this banging and crashing in the garden and, when I looked over the fence I saw Magenta trying to fasten these skates to the bottom of an old tray. You should've seen her – she was concentrating so hard she looked really sweet. But then, every time she stepped on the tray, it tipped up and walloped her on the leg. I stood there for ages, watching, but I don't think she realised. I felt so sorry for her but I was torn. Of course, the thing that was stopping me going and helping was the fact that I knew she was going to all that trouble for that stupid Ryan Dunn who, let's face it, doesn't give a monkey's about her. I'm sure he only asked her out because she's a bit of arm candy around school. He doesn't respect her (like I do) and he's not interested in any of the things she's interested in (like I am). He only wants her as a trophy and Magenta's too sweet and trusting to realise it. But I knew if I said any of those things to her she'd probably go mad and say I was jealous (which I'm not denying). Anyway, I couldn't stand watching her inflict injury on herself any longer so I offered her the one Dad got me when I was a kid.

'I've got my old skateboard in the shed if you want to borrow it.'

You should've seen her face – she was so grateful. And she was really worried about it getting damaged too. Anyway, she asked me to give her lessons so we went down the park and I'm telling you, we had the most amazing time. She was really wobbly at first and kept sort of falling sideways so that I had to catch her. And I'm pretty sure that sometimes she did it deliberately – you know, like she wanted me to put my arms round her and stuff like that. I just know that if it wasn't for that stupid Ryan Dunn, we'd be going out again. She made it obvious that she still likes me so I'm pretty sure she's only sticking with him because she doesn't know how to get out of it. I thought it might help if I told her about how I'd dumped Hattie on the Friday before the holidays – you know, give her a few ideas about how to do it.

I said to her, 'You know, Magenta, I was talking to Mum . . .' Magenta really rates my mum. I think it's because she hasn't got a mother of her own, so she sort of looks to my mum as a bit of a role model. '. . . and she pointed out that by going out with someone I wasn't totally into, I wasn't acting with integrity.' Magenta was pretending to concentrate on the skateboard, but I could tell she was taking it all in. 'So I finished with Hattie last night and it was amazingly easy. I just told her "You know, Hattie, this doesn't feel right – you and me." ' (What I didn't tell her was that we'd just been to the pictures and I'd spent the whole time wishing it was Magenta next to me and wondering if she was out somewhere with that plonker.) 'And then Hattie said she knew exactly what I meant. She told me she did like me and everything – as a friend – but she didn't think she was ready to go out with anyone else because she wasn't over Max yet. And you know what, Magenta? I feel so much better.'

And then Magenta nodded a bit, like she was thinking about what I'd said. 'Oh – that's good,' she said. Which has to be a positive sign. I mean, why else would she say it was good that I'd finished with my girlfriend? We were going to talk about it a bit more over a cup of tea but then the Dibners arrived and it was a case of 'Who let the dogs out?' big time. Unfortunately my skateboard got smashed up in the process but I didn't say too much because Magenta was upset enough about it. She's got such a sensitive nature. So when she was so quiet last Sunday, I really didn't know what was going on. I hoped she was mulling over the whole integrity thing with her and Ryan.

Justine was being the exact opposite of quiet though – talk about full on! 'Hey, can I check my e-mail on your computer, Daniel? I can't believe Uncle Curtis won't let Magenta go on the Internet, can you?'

'Erm, sorry, Justine but we're not on the Internet, either.'

'Oh, my God, you're practically prehistoric around here. How d'you manage? I don't know what I'd do without my e-mails and texts.'

'You can go to the Internet café in town to check them.' I looked at Magenta. 'We could take Justine to @titude one day next week, couldn't we?'

'What?' Magenta gave a big sigh. 'Yes, I suppose so.' Then, as though she'd just realised what had been going on, 'So, have you got your own e-mail?' She'd hardly spoken till then but suddenly she sounded really put out.

'Course!' Justine was flicking through my CD collection. 'I mean, take this Didier boy I met skiing, there's no way I'd be able to keep in touch with him if I didn't have e-mail.' Then Justine turned to me. 'I keep telling Magenta, she really ought to get a mobile. You must have one, haven't you, Daniel?'

'No, but I'm thinking of getting one.' Which was partly true. Magnus and his evil twin had got them and I could see there were definite advantages to being in contact but it hadn't really occurred to me to get my own until Justine asked.

'Didier? Who's Didier?' Magenta asked.

'That French boy I met on holiday – you know!'

'No, I don't know. What French boy? You never said anything about a French boy.' Magenta seemed really narked.

'Ooo, he's so gorgeous.' Now that was spooky. The way Justine said that was just like Magenta. 'But anyway, Daniel, I could go with you and help you choose a phone this week if you like. Mum and Dad did loads of research before they bought mine so I could advise you on the best deals and everything.'

'Justine!' Magenta was getting really agitated. 'What French boy?'

'Oh, he's soooo dreamy. His parents own the hotel where we stayed. Oooo, you should see him on the piste, Magenta – he's so professional. He's been skiing since he was about three. Honestly, you should ask Uncle Curtis and Belinda to take you skiing next year. It's brilliant.'

And then Magenta stood up. 'I have to go now. I've got to phone Ryan.'

'You could phone him from here if you had a mobile.' Magenta looked as though she was going to floor her but Justine seemed totally oblivious. 'So Daniel, have you thought what sort of phone you're looking for?'

And actually Justine and I had a really wicked week. I used my car-washing money and she went with me to buy a mobile, which is really cool. I've been texting Magnus all week. It's excellent. And I took her down to @titude most days (apart from Wednesday, when I got grounded and she went to the Leisure Centre with her dad and Holden). Spud and the lads were at @titude too and Justine got on really brilliantly with them. As well as checking her e-mail, we did a bit of surfing and stuff. I don't know if practical joking is in the genes but there was a little bit of it with Justine.

'Hey guys – check out the Lamborghini getting a ticket.' Then she waited for everyone to dash to the window. 'Fooled you!' I don't know why Magenta moans about her so much.

But, unfortunately for me, we didn't see much of Magenta all week. She spent the whole time helping her dad and gran with the preparations for the party. I was practically going potty with frustration but then, yesterday evening when Justine and I were playing on my computer, she came round to my room.

She looked really upset and I thought, this is it! She's dumped Ryan and she's come to ask me to take her back – as if she needed to ask!

'Daniel, can I talk to you?'

'Course you can.' Oh, this felt so good! It was just like the old days. 'Juss, would you mind?' I said and sort of flicked my head in the direction of the French windows.

'Sure. I'll go next door and see if the Chuckle Sisters want any help with the food. Later Madge!' Justine was OK about leaving us – she's very mature in a lot of ways.

Magenta sat on the edge of my bed and I was just longing to put my arms round her. 'Daniel, a terrible thing's happened. It's Belinda.' And she burst into tears.

'Hey, come on.' I didn't quite know what to do. I mean a few months ago it would've been OK for me to put my arm round her and comfort her but the whole splitting-up thing had put a question mark over that line of approach. But I didn't feel right just standing there watching while the girl that I loved was so upset. And, trust me, it's not often Magenta gets that upset about anything. I sat down next to her and faffed about a bit and then I remembered what Mum had said about being romantically spontaneous. What the hell! The situation couldn't really get any worse could it? So I put my arm round her and, the brilliant thing was, she let me – well, for a while anyway. Oh, she felt so soft and so vulnerable. It was like this huge aching crevasse had opened up in my chest. I'd missed her so much.

After a little while she pulled away. 'Belinda's leaving.'

'What?' This was awful. 'Leaving where? When?'

'Our school. She's going to be head of department at Archbishop Desmond Tutu in September.' Archbishop Desmond Tutu Technology College was right at the other side of town. This was a disaster. I mean, I wasn't taking Art next year, but Ms Lovell was the best Art teacher Archimedes High had. And she was just so brilliant doing the scenery for the play. 'She handed her notice in today – apparently she said it was such a difficult decision she left it right to the last minute and the Crusher was furious.' Then she started crying again. 'Oh Daniel, this is all my fault.'

'How is it your fault?'

'She says she's going so that it won't be so difficult for me. So that means, if I hadn't made all that fuss about my pottery she wouldn't be leaving.'

I put my arm round her again. 'Look, I don't know squat about teachers and their jobs but if she's had to hand her notice in today to start a new job after Easter, which is, what – two months away? Then it strikes me that she would've been applying for it a long time before you had your little pottery incident.'

Magenta sat up and looked at me. 'You know something, Daniel? You're right. She must've been planning this for ages. What a scheming cow!'

'Whoa!' *Now* where was she coming from? She stood up and made for the French windows. 'Hang on,' I said. 'Why're you mad?'

'Honestly, Daniel. Do try to keep up! Can't you see what she's doing? She's trying to make herself out to be Saint Belinda – sacrificing her job for my sake and then not saying anything until it's too late to talk her out of it. I'm going to go and have it out with her now. No way is she going to leave me in the lurch next year.' Wow! She looked so beautiful when she was angry.

Then just as she was leaving she turned round and said, 'Thanks, Daniel. I mean, really – thank you for being there for me.' She came back and sat back down on my bed. She smiled one of her fabulous smiles, like the Mona Lisa; all sexy and mysterious – with hardly any braces showing. Oh yes! This was it – she was going to say how much she'd missed me and how she regretted breaking up with me. I looked her straight in the eye and smiled back at her. My lips were already beginning to twitch in anticipation. 'You're a good mate, you know, Daniel. Can we be cool again?' And then she left.

Mates? Cool? No way! I wanted us to be hot again. I was gutted. What was I doing wrong? I'd been honest. I'd been myself. I'd been spontaneous *and* romantic. I didn't know what else I could do.

There was a bleeping telling me there was a text message on the mobile phone Justine and I had bought.

R U OK? Cn I cm ovr?

But before I could reply Justine knocked on my window. 'I love this arrangement you and Magenta have. It's so cool.' She came in and sat down right where Magenta had been two minutes earlier. Apart from their hair, the resemblance was uncanny.

'Is Holden with you?' I was braced, just in case.

'No, he's playing Pokémon with Dad and Uncle Curtis.'

'And Magenta?'

'She's talking to Belinda. You really like Magenta, don't you?' she asked.

Was it that obvious? 'Well – you know – a bit. I suppose.'

'Well, if it's any consolation I don't think she's that keen on this Ryan guy. She asked him to Uncle Curtis' party and . . . well, let's say he didn't sound too keen on the idea and she was peed off in the extreme.' It should've been music to my ears but I just sat there like a saddo. Was there any hope for the two of us? 'So, for the moment,' Justine went on, 'what do you say you change your game plan?'

'What?' I thought my mobile phone must've fried my brain already.

'Well, look at it this way – in twenty-four hours' time we're both going to a party on our own, right? My boyfriend's in France and, let's face it, there's not a whole lot of hope of the two of us going out again – ever. And you're not with anyone at the moment.' She gave her eyebrows a knowing twitch. 'So why don't we just make the most of the situation?'

'Erm . . .' I thought about what Mum had said. 'I don't know, Justine. I mean, do you think we'd be acting with integrity?'

'Who gives a monkey's about integrity?' she said and launched herself on to me. Wow! Who needs integrity when you can kiss like that?

The trouble was, some time in the middle of the night the big dream machine in my head had got reality and fantasy jumbled up and I ended up thinking that it had been Magenta on the end of my lips. And then the true horror had dawned that it wasn't either Justine or Magenta – it was the Grub complete with a soggy face cloth.

I leapt out of bed but forgot that he was sleeping on a mattress next to my bed and for some reason best known to the mother ship he had half the contents of Mum's sewing box on it. 'Ow! Ow! Ow!' I hopped about in agony trying to remove several pins that were dangling from my big toe.

'Ssssh!'

'Never mind "Ssssh", you little nerd. What're you doing with all this stuff on your bed? And what time is it, for heavens' sake?' I peered at my clock. 'Can't you tell the time yet, you little jerk? Look!' I pushed his face toward the glowing red digits that said 5:00. Now, you probably think that sounds a little harsh and, I have to be honest, I'm not usually in favour of cruelty to defenceless children or small animals – but as Holden doesn't come into either category, my conscience was clear.

'Listen.'

'What am I supposed to be listening to? It's the middle of the night and I've got half a tonne of steel in my foot – thanks to you!' Just then I heard the sound of an alarm going off and he started to giggle. 'Holden, what is going on?' Was I missing something here?

'I set Joe's clock forward two hours.' Oh great! This was all I needed. As if two black eyes weren't enough, Holden seemed to think I should go for the hat trick.

It was bad enough that we all had to suffer because Joe had got himself a Saturday job stacking shelves in the local Eight-till-late minimart in the High Street. This meant he was supposed to start work at seven-thirty – and didn't he let us all know it!

'Holden – you're on your own with this one.' I switched off the bedside light and leapt back under the duvet pretending to be asleep. I could hear the bathroom light go on and the door shut. The water was running for ages – he must've been having a shower.

'OK – wait for it,' Holden whispered. Wait for what? A firing squad?

I could hear Joe leave the bathroom and go back to his own bedroom. His radio went on. Surely he must've realised it was only quarter-past five?

Then I heard it – a sort of muted, strangulated scream followed by a crash.

'Holden! What've you done?'

The door to my room burst open and the main light went on. I rubbed my eyes and yawned as though I'd just woken up. 'Wazzup, Joe?'

'Wazzup? You know what's up.' Joe was standing in his boxers and T-shirt and he threw his jeans at me so that the legs wrapped themselves round my face – gross! 'That's what's up – you.'

At this point Holden poked his head up. 'Hi Joe! You're up early.'

Joe looked at the clock on my bedside table. 'Twenty-past five! Twenty-past five! I'm going to kill you, you . . .' He shot a glance at Holden who was sitting up with puppy-dog eyes (obviously been having lessons at the Macaulay Culkin *Home Alone* drama school) and toned down his insults. 'You sad excuse for a human being! Now unpick them.'

I hadn't a clue what he was talking about.

And then Holden began to chuckle. 'Akela taught me how to do it at Cub Camp last summer. You sew up the bottom of someone's trouser legs so that they fall over when they try to put them on. Good, isn't it?'

We both looked at him and suddenly I realised that, much as I could quite happily bury the little guy up to his neck in sinking mud, I didn't want his blood on my carpet so my first priority had to be to stop Joe mid-execution. As Joe lurched at Holden, I jumped forward and tackled Joe round the knees. Unfortunately, as he fell he knocked over the glass jar that was sitting on my chest of drawers. I watched in horror as it fell sideways. The rubber band that had been holding a piece of net curtain over the mouth twanged off and the jar smashed into a dozen pieces when it hit the edge of the speaker that was on the floor next to my bed. I couldn't believe it. Holden's colony of eighty-three stick insects (including babies) had just been released into the wild.

'I'm going back to bed, you little runt.' I wasn't sure which one of us Joe was speaking to. 'And I'd better not find a single one of those within ten feet of my bedroom or you're dead. Understand?'

8
Magenta

OK – now correct me if I'm totally wrong on this one but aren't parties supposed to be fun? I mean, doesn't the word conjure up images of people laughing and dancing and enjoying themselves? I know this could well be a generational thing – this is a parental party, after all, hardly the supercool, hip and trendy event of the decade – but, even so, I've had about as much fun this week as a turkey on the run-up to Christmas. (Or nut roast in my case.)

The reasons being:

1) Apart from one measly trip to the bus station (when I took a sneaky detour on the way home from the supermarket) haven't seen my (supposed) boyfriend all week.

2) The aforementioned (supposed) boyfriend was extremely rude when I invited him to Dad's party saying he didn't *do* parents and he hasn't phoned me all week or returned any of my calls.

3) I've spent the first part of the week incarcerated in the kitchen with Dad and Uncle Wayne playing Handy Andy to their DIY House Invaders.

4) And the second part of the week incarcerated in the kitchen with Can't Cook & Won't Admit I Can't Cook Gran while Auntie Heather sat on the sidelines giving us a running commentary on their skiing holiday – what I don't know about nursery slopes isn't worth knowing.
5) And I've had no privacy for the entire week because I've had to share my room with Ms I've-been-out-with-a-French-boy. (And doesn't she let us all know it – times a thousand!)

Plus, at quarter-past five this morning, it sounded like next door had been raided by the riot squad.

'What's going on?' I could hear all this shouting and then the sound of glass breaking.

'Ooo, let's go round there and see what's happening.' Justine was out of bed and through my French windows before I could even switch on the light. (Trust her – she'll go for anything French.)

'Justine – wait!' It was freezing out there and she was only wearing these stupid teensy little microscopic baby-doll pyjamas. I mean, call me Ms Sensible, but I'd rather be uncool than frozen to death, so I rummaged around for my dressing gown and fluffy slippers. (Unfortunately Sirius must've thought they'd been bought as playmates for him because what's left of them looks like they've been struck down with mange.) So, by the time I got over the balcony to Daniel's room I couldn't believe my eyes. My cousin Justine was standing with her arms round Daniel's neck – practically eating him in her disgustingly skimpy night-dress – while Holden was wolf-whistling at them and picking these evil-looking creatures out of the mess of broken glass and leaves that were all over the floor.

'Daniel!' I was shocked. I mean, I know Daniel and Justine have been getting on quite well this week but I didn't know they'd been getting on *that* well. There I was playing kitchen-maid to Gran and Auntie Venice and thinking how sweet Daniel was being, taking Justine out and saving me from having to hang out with her, when all the time he was snogging the socks off her. *And* he's only just finished with Hattie. *And* she's supposed to be going out with this boy from France. I mean, there are certain questions that come to mind here. Like:

a) Has he got no taste in girls at all?

and

b) What was all that rubbish he was spouting last week about integrity?

And to think that last night, after I'd been round there and confided in him all about Belinda and everything, I'd even started to think that I might have misjudged him on the whole older woman issue. Misjudged him, my foot! What a skunk he is! In fact, that just confirms what I've thought all along – that I really do want my next boyfriend to be older and more mature. I'm not going to mess around with these silly little Year 9 and 10 boys any more. I mean, even Adam Jordan was a total snake and he was Year 11, so it's sixth-form boys for me from now on.

'Jesus, Mary and Joseph! What in heavens' name is going on?' Mary was standing in Daniel's doorway in her dressing gown.

'Mum, I can explain everything,' Daniel said.

'You'd better!' She looked furious. 'Holden, leave that, you'll cut yourself. Girls, go back to your own room immediately and take Holden with you.'

'Aw, do I have to?' Holden had taken the words right out of my mouth. If there was one person in the world I would less like to share my room with than Justine, it was her doofus brother – especially if he'd got any of those disgusting twigs-with-legs attached to him. (No, actually, if there was one person in the world I would less like to share my room with, it was Daniel the Spaniel – slobbering all over every girl who gets within lip distance.) But I could see that Mary was in no mood for discussion, so I grabbed

Holden by the PJs. 'Save it, Germ-boy!'

As I was closing my French windows I could just make out Mary's voice. 'Start talking, Daniel – and this had better be good.'

I was still really peed off – a little bit with Holden for being such a . . . well, for just being Holden really. But mainly with Justine. 'He's your brother, Justine, so sort it out. I don't want him anywhere near me after he's been touching those things.'

But then, I hate to admit it, Justine actually went up a couple of rungs on my ladder of respect. She grabbed Holden by his pyjama neck and lifted him about two inches off the ground. 'You are *so* busted. Now spill.' When he'd finished telling her all about Joe's trousers (which, actually, I thought was a wicked trick – but I didn't say so in front of Holden), she rang Mary on her mobile.

'Mrs Davis? . . . Yes, it's Justine here . . . My brother has something he'd like to tell you.' And she handed him the phone. But, just when I thought she was doing the decent thing, she whispered to me, 'Well, the last thing I want is Daniel being grounded for the party, isn't it?' Gggrrrr! I mean, how manipulative is *that*? But, actually, if we go back to last Monday, you'll see that it's probably the perfect ending to a perfect week.

Now, I know the décor in the kitchen may not have been everyone's cup of tea with its dried-on clay motif but, personally, I thought it had a certain ethnicky charm to it. But oh no! Dad wanted it all repainted before his big day. Honestly, I don't know why he bothered. All that effort and he only went and painted it terracotta! I mean, it was half-way there anyway. But that's parents for you – always rushing to fix things when they're not even bust. And the worst thing was, for the whole of the first day he had me sanding the walls down till I looked like I'd fallen head-first into a vat of talcum powder.

'But your dad told me you had a certain affinity with sanding disks!' Did I say Uncle Wayne was cool? Well, I want to exercise my right to change my mind. Uncle Pain more like!

And after that they had me washing brushes in this gross, stinky stuff. It's no wonder I steered clear of Ryan for a few days. I mean, it hardly features in the book of 'One Hundred Ways to become a Boy-magnet', does it? Ditch the 'Eternity' and splash on a few gallons of 'Eau de White Spirit'.

Then, just when I thought I'd earned my freedom. . .

'Oh no, you don't! Your gran and Auntie Venice need a hand with the cooking!' Cell Block H, or what? It was all:

'Just chop these five sacks of onions, will you, Magenta love.' Like, hello! Don't they care about my eyes at all? Or do they just have shares in Kleenex?

And then:

'Just wash up those saucepans, there's a good girl.' Yeah – those saucepans that were piled so high Auntie Heather could probably ski down the north face of them. Plus, they'd been incinerated to a darker shade of charcoal – honestly, I don't know how Auntie Vee could let them get into that state – they were disgusting.

And then, talk about ungrateful! 'What on earth's happened to my saucepans?' Auntie Venice was staring at the draining board like she'd just had electric shock treatment.

'I've washed them up, like you asked me to.' I'd scrubbed so hard I'd practically worn my fingers to the bone and I'd used an entire box of Brillo pads to get that lot clean. The phrase *new pins* sprang to mind. 'It's taken me ages, Auntie Vee, honest: they were absolutely black.'

'They were *supposed to* be black! They had a non-stick coating!' Oops! 'That's why I brought them over, you silly . . .'

'Now Venice, love, Magenta's doing her best, aren't

you? She wasn't to know. Why don't you pop down to the minimart for me, love, and get me another half-dozen eggs? I haven't quite got the hang of these meringue things yet. And Heather, love, you never did finish telling us how Wayne managed to get his toggle out of the chair lift.'

That was when I managed to grab half an hour with Ryan – sorry, correction – I managed to grab about two minutes with Ryan and the other twenty-eight I spent sitting on a wall while he leapt and twisted and spun about like a . . . like a stupid leapy, twisty thing. In the end I was in danger of sinking into boredom-induced brain death, so I went off to buy Gran's eggs. She's got her heart set on making this pavlova pudding that she's seen on the front of a magazine. It looks all white and fluffy with huge great dollops of cream and massive juicy strawberries all over it. The trouble is, Gran's had four attempts so far – the first three came out of the oven in increasing shades of brown, from Jaffa cake through to distinctly char-grilled. Then the last one wasn't cooked long enough and dribbled all over the floor like pavlova à la PVA glue.

'Not to worry,' she said. 'We've got twelve lovely egg yolks for the quiches.' Personally, I wasn't convinced. I don't know about you but I think we'd have had more luck with the catering if Dad'd picked any one of the names from the list of top ten poisoners of all time.

Anyway, I went off to the minimart so that she could have another six 'lovely egg yolks for making quiches'. I could see that I was going to be eating quiche until my birthday at this rate. As I went past @titude on my way to the shops, I could see Justine in there in the middle of a group of boys. There was Daniel (and to think I was feeling *grateful* to him for looking after Justine!), Spud was there too and the Liable twins, Magnus and Angus. I know I'd moaned about having her down for the week but when I saw them all laughing and joking, I have to confess, I felt like a real loser. I mean, let's face it, could my week get any worse?

1) My boyfriend (soon to be ex-boyfriend, I'd decided) couldn't give a monkey's about me,

2) I couldn't see my friends because I was supposed to be making amends for the whole pottery-in-the-kitchen incident which, quite frankly, was ancient history as far as I was concerned,

3) I couldn't even speak to my mates on the phone because the over-thirties brigade had commandeered it every evening to 'finalise their party arrangements'.

On top of which

4) I had to put up with Justine and her, 'You should get a mobile, Madge, then you'd be able to speak to them' – ggggrrrrr!

And, as a final straw

5) There was the runner-up in the 'Irritation of the Year Award' herself, in the midst of Daniel and his crew – having a ball!

There is no justice in this world! I suppose the only consolation was that the *actual* winner of the 'Irritation of the Year Award' was being entertained by Dad and Uncle Wayne. This has to have been the all-time worst half-term since the invention of the holiday. The only good thing about it was that Gran said I could make Dad's birthday cake – and that was brilliant. He'd said he wanted a chocolate button cake and I found this recipe in an old 'We Can Cook' book Gran had bought me when I was little (ironic or what?). I'd just got to decorate it now and put the candles on. I felt really proud of myself. It didn't look quite like the photo in the book – in fact it would probably be difficult to tell it apart from any one of Gran's first three meringues – but I'm sure it would taste scrummy.

Sadly, though, there was a slight crisis on the

quiche front. (Although, maybe not *that* sad. In fact, pretty lucky from the packed lunch point of view.)

'Florence!'

'Yes, Venice, love? What's the matter?'

'What's in the oven at the moment?'

Gran looked at Auntie Vee like she was losing her marbles. 'You know what's in the oven. It's the quiches.'

'So, in that case, why are these still in the fridge?' Oops! Having accumulated an entire battery farm of egg yolks Gran had apparently sustained temporary amnesia and forgotten to add them to the milk and cheese mixture. The result was not a pretty sight – six extremely dubious looking pastry cases slopping about with hot milk and melted cheese – yuk!

'Look, Mum, it doesn't matter. There's lots of other food after all.' Dad was desperately trying to console Gran and stop her from going into a total decline. Poor Gran – she'd worked so hard. 'There's all those sausage rolls I saw you making yesterday . . .' Auntie Vee attracted his attention with a discreet cough and pointed to what looked like a bucket of coal by the back door. 'Wow! That trifle looks fantastic!' Nice try, Dad but, sadly, another wrong turn.

'Ooooooh! It's a packet mix to use up the cream because I couldn't manage the meringues.' And she ran out of the kitchen. Two minutes later she was back with her helmet on. 'Venice, give me the keys, will you? I need to get some air.'

And it was just at that point that Belinda chose to drop *her* little neutron bomb on the proceedings. Nice timing, or what?

So that, in a nutshell, has been my half-term. I need another week off to recover. And I'm not even going to mention Valentine's Day or the fact that the only cards I got were from Spud and Daniel – again! Even my dad had a more romantic Valentine's Day than I did this year. But never let it be said that I let an opportunity pass. I think I might have done a deal with Dad.

'OK – now the way I see it, you've got fifty people arriving at about eight o'clock tomorrow night and as things stand at the moment the only food you've got to offer is a trifle and a chocolate cake.'

'Just get to the point, Magenta.' I think he was a tad anxious because Gran still hadn't come back on the bike.

'Well, I'm willing to feed the five thousand for you, provided that . . .'

'Whoa! Before we have any *provided thats*, I want to know how you're planning on feeding fifty people? I am not paying for twenty-five pizzas to be delivered.' Honestly, parents are so suspicious.

'Well, I was thinking – sandwiches would be good.'

'Nice idea, love, but not quite what I had in mind for my birthday bash.'

'No, seriously, Dad, they're the food of the twenty-first century – 'Prêt à Manger' and all that.'

There was the merest hint of a chuckle. 'OK.' He still didn't sound convinced. 'So let's hear what this is going to cost me.'

And I told him. 'A mobile phone. It doesn't have to be anything flashy like a WAP-phone or anything like that. Just one that I can text my friends on, or use in emergencies – like when I got dumped by Adam Jordan last year or when I was late back from the park on Saturday.' And this is where I played my trump card. 'It'd mean you'd be able to check up on me.'

So he's thinking about it – which is always a good sign with Dad. Now all I have to do is ice his cake and make about a hundred rounds of sandwiches. No problem. Oh my God – catastrophe! I haven't even thought about what I'm going to wear!

'What d'you think?' Justine was standing in the middle of the sitting room with her troll-doll scaredo, wearing this cowhide two-piece and giving everyone a twirl.

'Oh, you look lovely, darling.' Auntie Heather must still be suffering from snow-blindness – it was the only possible explanation.

'Do you like it, Magenta?'

I mean, what could I say? Although the initials BSE were on the tip of my tongue.

Fortunately Gran came to the rescue. 'Very nice, Justine, love. Is that Friesian or Aberdeen Angus? I never can remember which one's which. Magenta, love, you need to go and put the chocolate and candles on your dad's cake. There are some buttons on the table and while you're in there will you sprinkle those flaked almonds on top of the trifle?'

Phew! Narrow escape. The trouble was, when I got into the kitchen, there was the Gremlin himself with chocolate all round his mouth and an empty packet of chocolate buttons. The disaster rate on this party was getting pretty close to catastrophe level and it was too late to buy any more.

'Just get out!' I screamed and made a mental note to ask Daniel if he'd noticed a 666 tattooed on Holden anywhere as he'd got undressed – that is, if Daniel could manage to prise himself off Justine for two seconds! But, in the meantime, it was a case of my creative talents to the rescue again. Someone (I think it might have been Spud, but we won't dwell on that) once told me that they have human tasters for pet food. If that was the case I was pretty certain that it must be true for doggie chocs too. There was no option. Dad wanted a chocolate button cake for his birthday, so a chocolate button cake he would get! And I was sure no one would notice the difference.

So the only thing left to do was locate the flaked almonds and sprinkle them on the trifle and then go and get changed – always the hardest part of any occasion. It was while I was upstairs, half way through getting dressed, that I heard it.

'Aaaaagh!' If I wasn't mistaken, it sounded very much like Gran, leaping off the edge of reason and plummeting into a total breakdown. I was sure that Holden must be scrabbling around at the bottom of it somewhere but then there was a knock at my door.

'Magenta?' It was Belinda. 'What did you put on the trifle?'

A fairly obvious question, but I thought I'd hazard a guess. 'The flaked almonds, like I was asked?'

'Do you know what flaked almonds look like?'

Did she think I was a total moron? 'Of course! They're those thin, creamy-coloured oval things that were on the table.' I could hear Gran's wailing reach a crescendo and I was getting the distinct impression that the blood-curdling scream from the kitchen was somehow connected to Belinda's line of questioning.

'OK, now I know this is not your fault . . .' which means that everyone is blaming me and Belinda's trying to be diplomatic '. . . but can you tell the difference between flaked almonds and sliced garlic?'

Uh oh! Gran's one and only contribution to her son's birthday blow-out had just joined the rest of her disasters in the bin and even though everyone was busy telling me it wasn't my fault, no one seemed to be telling Gran. She didn't speak to me all evening. As if that wasn't bad enough Holden and I seemed to be the only two people (apart from Gran and Auntie Venice) who weren't part of a couple, so Dad kept dragging me on to my feet and telling me to dance with the Grubling. *Plus* I was expected to sit and watch Justine chomping her way round my sitting room with her lips locked on to Daniel like a plunger on to a plughole! And, apart from that, the place was full of people who'd been trawled up from twenty years ago – it felt as though I'd wandered into some parallel universe that was locked in a fashion timewarp. I know Dad hadn't said it was a 1980s theme party but when you saw most of the guests, he might as well have done. What a nightmare! The only people who were even remotely of my generation were clamped on to each other like a pair of limpets on super-glue. Even the music was by artists who were so old they were practically dead.

Joe was doing the music so I went over to him. Any port in a storm, as they say. 'Can't you play something that's a bit more funky?'

'Your dad's given me the playlist.' Joe's not big on conversation.

'So, where's Anthea tonight then?' As if I cared where the Pritch was – so long as she wasn't here.

'Dunno. Gone out with her mates I expect.'

I was seriously in danger of slipping into a coma when Belinda came up and said something to Joe. Then the music stopped and Joe seemed to be transformed into MC Mix Master Genius – completely inappropriately, I might add! 'OK everybody, let's big it up for the Daddy of Cool; the birthday boy himself. Who da man?'

One or two feeble voices piped up, 'Curtis da man.' I wanted to die with embarrassment. Then everyone started cheering as Uncle Wayne came in carrying the doggie choc birthday cake. '. . . Happy birthday de-ar Curtis. Happy birthday to you!'

I'm sorry but that was too much. It was definitely time for me to make a hasty exit. Apart from the fact that there may well be some weirdo who was a connoisseur of doggie chocolate and would suss me out (nothing would surprise me about my father's friends after that party), I just needed to get out of there before I totally fell off my perch. I was in need of some serious sanity and Seema was the one to sort me out.

Now, I know it was late but she only lives round the corner and I reasoned that if I took Sirius with me, he'd protect me from any mad axe-men lurking in the hedgerows.

'Magenta? Are you OK?' Seema was peering out from behind the chain on their door.

'Are your parents in?' The last thing I wanted was Mr and Mrs Karia to get the wrong impression of me like Arlette's parents had done.

'No, they've gone over to my auntie's, why? What's the matter?'

'Everything! Can I come in?'

Unfortunately, I'd forgotten that Seema's brother, Sunil is allergic to dogs. 'Hang on till I get my coat and we'll walk round the block.' Seema's such a good mate. As we were walking I was telling her all about my horrible half-term. It all came pouring out, like an upset stomach.

'So what're you going to do?'

'What can I do? I mean, I can't tell Daniel who he can and can't go out with, can I?'

Seema looked at me a tad oddly. 'I meant, what're you going to do about Ryan?'

'Oh, him!' I have to confess, I'd got so screwed up about Daniel and Justine that the small matter of my boyfriend had slipped my mind. 'Well, dump him, obviously.'

'Good! You're worth so much more than that loser, Madge – honestly. And speaking of losers, look over there!'

We were passing the school gate and Seema pointed out that all the security lights were on around the quad. I think Fred, the caretaker, must've been out because we could hear his two German Shepherds, Saracen and Spartacus, going totally ape in the keepers' lodge. Sirius was practically crawling up my leg in fear so I picked him up and carried him – so much for being my guard-dog against marauding axe-men!

'Talk of the devil!' Seema said and pointed to a group of boys about a hundred metres away skateboarding on makeshift ramps that they'd constructed all round the quadrangle in the school grounds. 'OK, you said you wanted to dump him – so, no time like the present.'

'What, now?'

'Yep!'

'In front of all that lot?'

'You can do it.' And she took my arm, dragging me off towards the fence behind the Science block. There was a part that got broken down when Billy O'Dowd did a runner after he broke into the technician's prep room, nicked old Smelly's packed lunch and swapped it for the Year 8 investigation into growing mould.

'Seema, are you sure this is a good idea?'

'It'll be cool. Come on.' It was pitch dark behind the Science block and Sirius was being a total wuss. We waded our way through the sea of crisp packets that had blown into the corner – it was so gross. I wished Seema had thought to bring a torch. And I was sure I could hear someone behind us.

'You're paranoid.'

'Seema, can't this wait till Monday?'

'Look, we're here now. And the sooner you dump the low-life the sooner you can get sorted out with Daniel again.'

What a shocker! 'I don't want to get back with

Daniel again! Why would I want to swap one rat for another?'

'So why're you so mad that he's got off with your cousin?'

'What is this – *In the Psychiatrist's Chair*?' We'd rounded the corner and were looking at the quad, floodlit by the security lights that kept flashing on when anyone moved – which was pretty much all the time really. 'I do *not* believe it!'

'What?'

'Slapper Pritchard – there on the wall.' Anthea 'the Pritch' Pritchard, Joe's girlfriend, was sitting on the wall next to one of the home-made wooden ramps, examining the ends of her synthetic braids – either that or she was looking for her brain cell. And then Ryan skated up to her. He put his arm round her neck and pulled her towards him and then he only went and kissed her. My boyfriend (I know I'd decided to finish with him but he didn't know that yet) kissing the slapper to end all slappers! I was furious. I was just about to storm over there and tell both of them what I thought of them when three things seemed to happen at once:

1) There were a series of mini explosions from the skating ramps and people started falling off their skateboards.

2) Saracen and Spartacus bounded out of Fred the caretaker's house ready to eat anything in their path and making more noise than the hounds of the Baskervilles. And before you could say *Werewolf Alert*, naturally Sirius was up in my arms quivering like a jelly in an earthquake.

And, most worrying of all,

3) Three police cars screeched into the staff car park and, as the skaters ran in every direction, police officers ran after them.

'Now look what you've done!' I whispered to Seema. We shuffled back behind the corner of the Science block and I was hoping that we could retreat surreptitiously before anyone saw us.

'Me? How is this my fault?' Why do all my friends try to wriggle out of taking responsibility for their actions?

'Because it was your idea to come here.'

And then I heard it – one of the police men shouted, 'Hey, Sarge, this one can't be more than about eight or nine.'

I felt as sick as a parrot. I poked my head back round the corner and sure enough, there was the Stick Insect himself being frog-marched across the quad towards the police cars. I pushed Sirius into Seema's arms.

'Here, take Sirius and go and get Dad. Quick!' It was time to do the noble thing and give myself up to the police for the sake of the brat. Stuff stupid Ryan Dunn! Stuff Slapper Pritchard! It didn't matter that they seemed to have got away. As I walked across the yard towards the quad, Saracen and Spartacus snarling at me like they hadn't been fed in weeks, I knew that this was a far far better thing than anything I'd ever done before.

Not sure Dad was going to see it that way though.

9
Seema

I love Magenta to pieces – really I do. I mean, we've got a history that has its roots right back in nursery. But, honestly, sometimes! Take last Saturday for instance.

Now, my mum and dad are OK about me going out with boys – I mean, they're not over the moon about it, but they've come to terms with it. Actually, my parents are pretty OK. I'm the youngest of four, so it's like, 'Been there, done it, sat up all night worrying about it and have the emotional scars to prove it.' They had all their nervous breakdowns with my sister and brothers. I mean, when my sister Reena was my age, I was only just born, so I don't remember much about it but apparently she did the works; wild parties, English boyfriends, cut her hair off – you name it, she rebelled against it. But she's come through OK and now she's a high-powered, jet-setting computer whizz-kid, bombing off all over the world to 'trouble-shoot network problems'. I haven't a clue what that means except that she's not around much.

Then there's my brother, Anish. Anish is in his final year at uni and he's doing fashion design – which is so *not* what Mum and Dad had in mind for him. You should've heard the rows when all that was happening. But, once they could see how happy he was, they came round. So, really, I think they've pretty well exhausted all their parental anxieties by now – which can only be good for Sunil and me. In fact, I've got to be honest, I think they're pretty laid-back as parents go. But not so laid-back that they didn't hit the roof on Saturday.

I'd told them that I didn't want to go to Pooja Massi's because Hayden was coming round, which they were fine about. I mean, it wasn't like we were going to be in the house alone: Sunil was here too. Anyway, it was about ten o'clock and Hayden had just left.

'For heavens' sake, Suni, give it a break.' He's doing his A-levels this year so he's being a complete anorak about studying. 'Come and watch a video with me or something. I'm bored.'

'Hang on a minute then – I'm a bit wheezy, I just need to get my inhaler.' He'd disappeared upstairs when there was a knock on the door.

'Are you expecting anyone?' It was a bit spooky having someone at the door that late on a Saturday night – I mean, it's not the most sociable time to go visiting.

'I'll be down in a second. It's probably Raj, but put the chain on just in case.' Sunil's mate, Raj, comes round sometimes and they get into these really heavy conversations about the meaning of life and things like that. It all sounds a bit pretentious to me but Suni's going to do Philosophy next year so he justifies it that way.

But I couldn't believe my eyes when I opened the door. It wasn't Raj at all; it was Magenta. 'Madge!' She looked awful – as though she was going to burst into tears any second. 'Are you OK?'

'Can I come in?' Normally I'd have said yes, no problem, but she'd got Sirius with her and Suni's allergic to dogs.

'I take it it wasn't Raj?' Suni said, looking at Magenta. 'So I won't be needing this, then.' He waved the book he'd brought downstairs. *Kierkegaard and the Origins of Existentialism* – unless you're into existentialism, Magenta?' I know my brother's brainy but he can be a real show-off at times – he knew Madge wouldn't know anything about some hundred-year-old Danish philosopher but he just had to try and be smug.

'Oh absolutely!' Suni and I both looked at her for

signs of blagging but she was being totally serious. 'I hate prejudice of any kind, whether it's against humans or extra-terrestrials.'

And that's why I love her so much! 'Erm . . .' I could see Suni looking totally perplexed.

'But I didn't know you were a Trekkie, Sunil. That's great!'

'No . . . er . . . you see, Kierkeg . . .'

'Don't worry about it,' I said to Sunil. I was fairly sure she hadn't come round to discuss either philosophy or the Starship Enterprise so I grabbed my coat and took her arm. 'Come on, Madge, tell all.'

'Where're you going? You can't go out this late. What happens if Mum and Dad come home?'

'We're just going to walk round the block for a little bit. We'll only be about ten, fifteen minutes max. Is that OK?' He didn't look too happy about it but he's a sweetie underneath all his hot air. 'Cheers, bruv.'

Poor Magenta! She does manage to get herself into some messes. I know she'll never admit it but I'm sure she's still got the hots for Daniel. She didn't stop going on about him and her cousin and then, almost as an afterthought, she said she was going to finish with Ryan.

'About time too!' We'd just about reached the

bottom of the road where the school is. 'And speak of the devil – look who's over there.' Ryan and a gang of skaters had got into the school grounds and built all these makeshift ramps in the quad. It was obvious that Fred the caretaker wasn't in because his two pet wolves were practically tearing his house to pieces. I have to confess, I'm not the world's greatest dog lover and I gave a shudder when I heard them. 'Honestly, Madge, he's such a loser. And let's face it, it's hardly been the romance of the decade, has it?'

She looked a bit hurt and I thought maybe I'd been too blunt but then she set off very determinedly down the road. 'You're right! Come on then,' she said, 'no time like the present.'

I couldn't believe what she was thinking. 'What, are you going to go in there now?'

'Why not?'

'Well, the trespass laws, for one thing.' I did think it was a bit risky going on to the premises but my main objection, if I'm being honest, was Fred and his killer canines – who only seemed to be restrained right now by a very flimsy pane of glass and what seemed to me a negligently inadequate chain-link fence. I remember reading that animals can smell fear – well, I'm afraid in that case, I might as well have drenched myself in 'Abject Terror' and sent out an invitation to 'Eat me please'. I could just about cope with Sirius but if the frenzied fiends broke free the only future I could see for any of us was as meat on feet.

'Oh trespass shnespass!' she said. 'It'll be cool. Come on.' And she led me round by the back of the Science block where the fence is down.

I was really not happy about the whole business but what could I do? There was no way I wanted to go home on my own at that time of night. So I decided to appeal to Magenta's rational, reasonable side – momentarily forgetting that she doesn't have one.

'Can't this wait till Monday? You can dump him at break in front of all his mates. That would be so much more effective than here in front of . . .' As we rounded the corner I peeked round and saw the quad, illuminated like the pitch at Old Trafford. There must have been twenty people there. So much for my argument – Ryan wouldn't be able to muster twenty friends at school if he was giving away free cup final tickets. I decided to give it one last shot. 'Look, it's never a good idea to rush into things. Why don't you go home and try and sort things out with Daniel?'

'Daniel? Why would I want to sort things out with

Daniel?' We were both whispering but Magenta was whispering much more loudly than I was.

'Well, you seem upset that he's got off with your cousin, I just thought . . .'

'Well, don't think, Seema. OK? Why anyone would want to swap one dirt bag for another is . . .'

And then Magenta pointed across the quad. There, sitting on the wall (with her mouth stuck on to Ryan Dunn like a suction pump) was Magenta's arch-enemy Anthea Pritchard herself. Uh oh! My primary objective now was to get Magenta out of there before she completely lost the plot and made a total prat of herself.

'Let's go, Magenta. Do this at school.' I'd just turned back towards the hole in the fence, when all hell let loose. There were sirens and lights and bangs and barking and dogs and policemen and people running and skateboarding in every direction. 'Quick! Let's get out of here.'

'Now look what you've done!' Magenta said to me as we picked our way through the rubbish behind the Science block.

'Me?' I was speechless. I mean, how did she work that one out?

'This was such a stupid idea!'

I was really annoyed with her actually. 'Madge, I

agreed that it was a good idea to dump Ryan – not break into school at the dead of night. Now let's go!' I grabbed her arm and started to pull her towards the broken fence. But as soon as we heard one of the policemen shouting about having caught an eight year old, Magenta went rigid.

'Oh – my – God! It can't be!' She went back and sneaked a look round the corner. 'Oh my God – it is!' She pushed Sirius into my arms. 'Here! Go and get Dad – quick!'

'Magenta, wait!' But she didn't. The last thing I saw of her she was walking across the quad with her hands in the air as though John Wayne was going shoot her in the back. I really don't know why Mr Grimsby doesn't like her – she could make a drama out of a tea bag. Anyway, Sirius gave a little whimper which might as well have rung the doggie dinner bell for the hounds from hell. As soon as they heard him they turned in our direction – which was my cue to get out of there and run like the clappers to fetch the cavalry. Luckily Magenta's house is almost as close to the school as mine. But when I got there, it was at the same level of pandemonium as the chaos I'd just left. People were out on the pavement; there was a police car there and a WPC was taking details from a woman who could only be Madge's Auntie

Heather. Her Dad was just getting into his car and her gran was dressed in leathers and was putting on her helmet.

'Mr Orange! Mr Orange!' I panted. Thank goodness they heard me.

'Seema! What. . .?' He got out of the car and then he saw Sirius. 'Oh no! Where's Magenta? What's happened?'

The woman that I thought must be Madge's auntie began to scream. 'Holden! My baby!'

'It's OK,' I said. 'They're both fine.'

'Thank heavens for that. So where are they?'

I was suddenly aware of everyone looking at me. I wasn't quite sure how to put it to cause the least distress but in the end I just decided to go for it. 'They've been arrested.'

And then Madge's aunt began screaming again. 'Oh, this is too much. Curtis, you have got to get that little minx under control.'

'This is not the time, Heather,' said a man who looked the spitting image of Magenta's dad.

'It's always the time for discipline, Wayne,' she was shouting over her shoulder as Magenta's gran led her indoors.

The WPC was on her walkie-talkie and people were generally drifting off.

'Great party, Curtis.'

'Yeah, happy birthday, Curtis!' I felt a bit sorry for him, actually. I mean, it's not the ideal birthday present, having your thirteen-year-old daughter arrested, is it?

'If you've been drinking, sir, I'd suggest you come down to the station with me,' the police officer said. 'And I think it would be a good idea for you to come too, as you seem to be the only witness,' she said to me.

As I was getting into the police car Daniel rushed out and grabbed my arm. 'She is all right, isn't she?'

'Sure. She's fine.' I wish Magenta would get over herself and go out with him again. And then I glared at this punky girl who'd come and put her arms round Daniel from behind. 'Magenta's such a star. She did it to protect her little cousin, you know?' I said, pointedly.

'Wow! My brother, the convict. How cool is that?' she said over his shoulder and I knew exactly what Magenta meant about her cousin.

Anyway, it all got sorted out in the end. It turns out that Magenta's cousin Holden had followed us down there and had then been shooting exploding caps out of a pellet gun at the skaters. Plus someone across the road had rung the police and they'd arrived at the same time as Fred and his wife had got home from bingo. Holden got off with a warning this time and good old Madge got commended for her part in trying to break up the trespassers. (I'm not quite sure how that came about, but there you go!) Unfortunately, by the time we all got back from the police station it was nearly one o'clock in the morning and my parents were not overly impressed. I mean I had phoned them and everything but even so, they've said I have to go with them to Pooja Massi's every Saturday from now on, which is a real bummer.

Of course there was a riot on Monday between Joe Davis and Ryan Dunn over Anthea Pritchard. I honestly wonder about boys. I mean, why do they go out with her when they know that she's almost guaranteed to two-time them? But anyway, Magenta's well out of that one. The trouble is now, she's totally setting her sights on Darien Quinn and, I daren't tell her this, but the more I work with him at rehearsals, the more I'm starting to fancy him. I know it's stupid because he's so much older than I am but he is quite hunky when he wriggles his hips and pouts. And then we have to kiss right at the end. We've only rehearsed it once so far but it was amazing. I mean, we kept it professional and everything, so it's not like there were tongues involved but, even so, I went all weak at the knees. I think Hayden was a bit put out at first but he gets to kiss this Year 11 girl, so he can't complain too much. I'm really enjoying the rehearsals – I'm so grateful to Magenta for suggesting it. There's another tonight and I can hardly wait.

What a fiasco! We were doing the beginning of the play: the scene where the boys and girls are doing their two-part song at either side of the stage. Ms Lovell's doing the sets and props and she'd got some of her team to bring one of the picnic tables in from the lower school playground. That was at one side of the stage and we were doing the bit where the girls were supposed to be having their lunch while I tell them about the dreamy guy I met on holiday. At the other side of the stage was a tiered set of PE benches for the boys to do their dance on. It's supposed to represent the seating round an athletics track.

'All right, now this is just a temporary measure until I can get some scaffolding arranged for the actual production.' Ms Lovell shook the back tier of benches. 'It's quite stable but just be a little bit careful. And girls, that bench is the one that rocks. We'll get it changed for next time but just remember to keep the weight balanced at each end for now. OK?'

I know all my moves but I'm a bit shaky on some of the words so we had to run through bits more than once and getting the timing between the two groups right was a bit tricky. The scene starts with Lou (the Year 11 girl who's playing Rizzo) sitting at the picnic bench with Nadine and Becki (who play Joan and Marty), and then Arlette and I have to come in and sit down with them.

'Anyone seen Nadine today?' Mr Marlowe was shouting as we took up our places.

'She's off today, Sir,' someone said.

'OK then, I'll need someone to stand in for her today. Er, Magenta, will you come and sit in for Nadine? You'll be playing Joan.' I grinned at her and gave her the thumbs up. Normally poor old Madge just hangs around in the background doing not very much, so I was glad that she'd got the chance be with us. I secretly hoped that if she was good, she might get one of the minor roles so that she had a little bit more prominence.

But then Mr Grimsby shouted, 'Just until Nadine's better, though. All right?' He was sitting at the back of the hall, 'taking an over-view', as he called it. I think he fancies himself as some hotshot Hollywood director.

Anyway, we'd gone through the scene about four times and even though I'd got my words right, Darien kept fluffing his. Ms Keyes was working with him while the rest of us were just sitting waiting. It was so nice to have us all there at the picnic table – including Magenta.

'He is gorgeous, isn't he?' she said, leaning across the table and smiling at Darien. I thought diplomacy was probably better than truth in this instance, so I didn't say anything.

'Well, if you ask me, he's up his own bum and I wouldn't touch him with a ten-foot pole,' Arlette said and then turned her gaze up at the lighting box. It didn't take a genius to work out who she was looking at. 'Has your cousin gone home now?'

'Yes – thank goodness. But now Daniel's got his mobile she's texting him every other minute. Honestly, I was round there last night and she must've texted him about ten times in the space of an hour. I mean, how pathetic is that?'

I thought Arlette looked a bit upset. 'Are you and Daniel back together again, then?'

'Nooooooo! Honestly, why does everyone keep going on about me getting back with Daniel? I am not interested! OK?'

'Girls, will you keep the noise down!' Ms Keyes

was getting a bit impatient. 'Right, Darien, take it from where you start to walk down the tiers. And the other T-Birds go with him. Off you go.'

Darien put his hands on his hips and cocked his head on one side. 'Well, you know, Ms Keyes, when my mother was at the Palladium . . .'

'He's sooo gorgeous, don't you think?' Magenta whispered.

'Darien, you are not your mother and this is not the Palladium. I really don't find these references terribly helpful. Now, if you could just take it from where you're standing at the top.'

'Oh, poor Darien.' And then Magenta sighed. 'Actually, I'm getting a bit bored. Whose magazine is that?'

'Mine,' said Lou.

'Can I have a look at it while we're waiting?'

'Sure,' Lou said without thinking.

'No!' I whispered as loudly as I dared. But it was too late. As Magenta stood up to go and fetch the magazine, the picnic table became unevenly balanced and suddenly tipped up. Arlette and Becki had been sitting at opposite sides of the table at the other end, so as our end of the table sprang up, theirs crashed to the floor and they slid down the seating and tumbled on to the stage in an inelegant heap.

Lou, who'd been in the middle, gave a little shriek and fell on top of them. But I'd been sitting opposite Madge at the other end of the bench. As Magenta had stood up, I'd been jolted upwards – not so violently that I was thrown off but I definitely rose several inches into the air. I came back down with a bump when the bench crashed to the normal position again, banging my elbow on the table and getting my foot caught under the leg of the bench as it hit the floor.

'Ow!' I couldn't help crying out, as much from shock as anything else.

Unfortunately Hayden, who's playing Kenickie, saw what had happened and panicked. 'Seema! Are you OK?' He leapt off the stack of PE benches at the other side of the stage, giving a perfect demonstration of Newton's Second Law of Motion. (Normally I get very excited when I can actually see Physics in action, but on this occasion it was more like watching the Chaos theory at work!) As Hayden pushed himself forward, he knocked the top bench backwards and created a sort of avalanche of benches. Unfortunately Darien had just started his little dancey bit, walking down the stepped benches. I watched as he wobbled, then grabbed one of the other boys to try and steady himself – sadly, not very successfully. There was a vaguely synchronised wobbling of T-Birds before they all fell over in a mass Humpty Dumpty effect. The chorus, who were standing in the wings, and the stage-hands, who were sitting in a group with Ms Lovell, all made a dash for it but not before one or two of them got caught in the flying debris of bodies and benches. It was more like a scene from *Earthquake* than *Grease*!

Once the dust had settled it went eerily quiet (except for the odd moan and a couple of rude words from Mr Marlowe). Hayden came across and put his arms round me.

'You OK, hon?' He's so sweet.

'I'm fine.' My toe was throbbing and my elbow felt as though someone had hit it with a hammer but I didn't want to make too much fuss – not when I looked round and saw the state of everyone else. People were generally rubbing their bumps and bruises but, fortunately, no one seemed to be seriously injured. Magenta was standing on the edge of the stage with Lou's magazine clutched to her chest. Her eyes were very wide and she was biting her bottom lip.

'Oops!' I heard her say under her breath.

'Right then!' Mr Grimsby stood up from his position at the back of the hall and began to walk down the aisle towards the stage. He had that unexploded bomb look about him.

'Mr Marlowe, if you'd be so kind as to supervise the clearing up, I think we'll call it a day.' He'd reached the front of the hall by now and was standing right in front of the stage. His face was a sort of deepish maroon colour and his eyes had gone very narrow. 'Hayden West – my office, first thing tomorrow morning.' Poor Hayden, I hoped he wasn't going to get told off just because he'd been concerned about me. Then Mr Grimsby turned his attention to Magenta. 'And as for you – my office – NOW!'

10
Magenta

At long last my life has started to look up. And the reasons for this little oasis of joy after such a desert of stress and anxiety for the past three months are as follows:

1) I finally managed to get out of doing the stupid school play. To be honest, I was only staying in the cast to keep Seema and Arlette company at rehearsals, so when the Grim Reaper tried to blame me for Hayden West wrecking the set, it was the final straw.

2) I'm working in the set and props team now which is so much more suited to my natural creative genius. Everything's coming together and I'm really enjoying it. It's the dress rehearsal next Thursday and I feel so proud when I look at what Belinda and I – and some other people, of course – have created.

3) Which brings me to the fact that Belinda and I understand each other so much better now after our little talk. In fact, I'm secretly hoping that she and my dad might decide to get married fairly

soon. Don't say anything but I'm going to see what I can do to help things on their way in that direction.

Away from school, things are looking up too.

4) Daniel and I are back to being good mates again, which is such a relief. I mean, it was all very convenient to have a boyfriend next door and everything but it's so much better to have a friend-friend – you know, so that the romantic stuff doesn't get in the way.

And, wait for this one, right –

5) DAD ONLY WENT AND BOUGHT ME A MOBILE PHONE! How amazing is that? He only gave it to me at the weekend mind you, so I'm still a bit of a novice. Daniel says he'll show me how to program people's numbers into the memory so that I don't have to try and remember everyone's when I want to text them. Not that that's an issue at the moment because Arlette and Seema haven't got phones so that does limit the number of people I can text. But not to worry because:

Majorly, majorly, mega-fantastic reason to be so ecstatically happy that I might actually float up and cause serious problems for air-traffic controllers everywhere:

6) DARIEN HAS ASKED ME OUT! Didn't I tell you that once he'd got to know me and seen how mature I was, he'd forget about the age difference?

I mean, this is hot off the press – it only happened a couple of hours ago! And the way he did it was so hi-tech and sophisticated. Listen to this, he only asked me out by text! How cool is that? Arlette and I had gone into town after school because she has to have this gross pink cardigan for the play and she couldn't face buying it on her own or with her mum in case anyone thought she was serious. So there we were in the middle of the old ladies' department (honestly, even my gran wouldn't be seen dead in half those clothes) when I got a text message. Now, I haven't been exactly inundated with calls in the five days since I've been an upwardly mobile girl about town. In fact, the only ones I've received have been from Dad or Gran asking me where I am. Oh, and Daniel on Monday morning – which I could have done without. *Hi! Howz my fave txt girl*? ☺ Which would've been really sweet of him except that mobiles are illegal at school and it arrived just as I was trying to explain to old Bonsie about my homework. (I was telling him the one where my dog had had a fit and eaten my essay before running out into the garden and rolling it around in the mud, which, of course, had meant that I'd had to completely re-write it from scratch! I must remember to make a note that I've used that excuse with him. I nearly got caught out last term when I told Mrs Blobby the one about falling over and spraining my wrist two weeks running! Actually, I think I should keep a little diary of what I've said to who and when. Wow! What a stroke of genius! I can cross-reference dates and teachers to make doubly sure I don't get confused! Brilliant – I wonder if I could patent the idea?) But anyway, to go back to Monday, I think I'd probably have got away with it if it hadn't been for Daniel's text but instead, I ended up having my phone confiscated on my first day. I was so mad with Daniel I told him not to text me again unless it was an emergency.

So, there we were in the middle of geriatric fashions, when off it went. Even though I knew it would be Dad, it was still pretty cool to be getting text messages in public. But when I looked at the little display, it was all written in proper text talk – not the standard English messages Dad sends! *CS ThnknAU* it said. Now, as I told you, I'm a bit of a novice texter so I did a double take. 'Uh? What's this supposed to mean when it's at home?'

'Let's have a look.' Arlette took my phone off me. 'Wow, it says, **"Can't stop thinking about you."** ' Arlette's sister, Cassie, is heavily into texting her mates from uni, so Arl's up on all the lingo. ' **"Will you go out with me?"** Wow, Madge! That's amazing!'

I could hardly believe what she was saying. 'Let me see. Give it back.' Sure enough, that's what it said. I could hardly believe it. This was so exciting. Then I had an awful thought. 'It doesn't say who it's from. It's probably Spud – or someone playing a joke.'

'Well look at the number then. Honestly, Madge, you're going to have to learn to use this or you'll look a complete dork. Do you recognise the caller number?'

'Noooo!' How was I supposed to recognise it when I don't know anyone's number yet?

'Well who knows yours?'

'Just about everybody.' I'd gone to the machine in the stationery shop and had fifty business cards printed with my number on. I'd given them to practically everyone I'd come into contact with in the last week.

'Great! Well, there's no option then, you'll just have to ring the number and find out who your mystery admirer is.'

Aaaaggh! No way! She couldn't really expect

me to ring up a total stranger and ask him if he'd asked me out. That's nearly as scary as pressing the 3 straight after doing 1471 before you've waited to hear who it is. But before I could object she'd grabbed my phone again and was busy ringing the number. Then she pushed it back into my hand. I have to say, I think Arlette's getting a teensy bit on the bossy side since she got the part of Frenchy. Personally, I don't think it's done her any favours.

'Hi, M- g- nta? Is – at you?' The voice sounded very familiar but it was a really bad connection and kept breaking up.

'Who is that?' This was creepy. It was obviously someone who'd got my number on memory because it'd come up on caller ID.

'It's me. Da—en.' I could not believe my ears! I put my hand over the mouthpiece and whispered to Arlette. 'It's him! It's Darien!'

'NOOOOooo!' Arlette mouthed back.

I nodded. 'Yes!' Then I went back to my phone. 'Wow, Darien, this is great.'

'You'll--ve to sp—k up. I'm on a bus and ---k—ps br---king up. C-n I t-k --- you later?'

My knees were going like a couple of crème caramels on a spin drier and my tummy was doing back flips. This was too wonderful for words. 'Course

184

you can. I just wanted to say, yes, I'd love to go out with you.' But we lost the connection about half-way through so I wasn't sure how much of it he'd caught. I grabbed Arlette's arm and started flapping it up and down. 'Oh my God, Arl! I can't believe it!' We were hugging each other and jumping up and down. Unfortunately we jumped up and down right across the aisle and into one of those chrome racks that had all these gross corsetty-looking things on it. I didn't realise but one of the hangers got caught on the strap of my schoolbag so that as we jumped away again, the whole rack came toppling over. It landed on top of us and we were buried underneath a mountain of hideous white, black and disgusting flesh-coloured lycra! Yuk! I think any one of them would have given an uplift to a fair-sized hippo and you could've made about twenty of my bra and knicker sets out of just one of them.

Unfortunately we got asked to leave after that, so Arlette never did buy her cardigan. But I'm home now and I still can't believe it. I'm just waiting for Darien to phone. Mind you, when I told Dad, he went into outer space on a turbo-boost of parental over-protection. I was sitting on the stairs and I could hear him and Belinda having a humungous row. I've never really heard them row before, so it was a bit worrying. And it was even worse because it was about me. I hoped it wasn't going to spoil their wedding plans.

'I don't care if he's up for RSC Actor of the Year Award, I am not letting my thirteen-year-old daughter go out with a sixteen year old.'

'I believe he's seventeen now.' Cheers, Belinda! Not doing my case a lot of good!

'Oh – and that's supposed to make me change my mind is it? The fact that he's now *four* years older than she is.'

'Don't be absurd, Curtis!' Oops! Not the best way of getting Dad round to her way of thinking. Magenta will be fourteen in a few months anyway. What I'm saying is, he seems a nice boy. Very mature and responsible.'

'A nice, very mature and responsible, *se-ven-teen-year-old*.' There he goes again with his talking in syllables.

'Oh, come on, Curtis. Look at some of the wallies she's been out with who were nearer her age. Compared to some of them, Darien's positively Prince Charming.' Cheek! I detected the slightest hint of criticism in there about my choice of boyfriends so far.

'What was wrong with Daniel? *He* was her age!'

Why does everyone keep going on about Daniel, for heavens' sake?

'Nothing was wrong with Daniel, they just didn't hit it off. You can't choose Magenta's boyfriends for her, Curtis.' Thank you, Belinda!

'Maybe not, but I can choose who's *not* going to be her boyfriend! So don't try to tell me how to bring up my daughter.'

'I'm not trying to tell you how to bring up your daughter. I'm not trying to *tell* you anything.' Belinda's voice had gone up about an octave. 'I was simply trying to offer an objective viewpoint but as you don't seem remotely interested in objectivity, I'm going to go home until we can discuss this reasonably!'

I started to scuttle back upstairs to my room but just then my phone went again, *1 New Message – Read Now?* And it was from the same number! Oh, I was torn. I really wanted to read the message and yet I also wanted to catch Belinda before she went home. I knew that if I could only talk to her, she and Dad would be able to make up. Now let me see: *my* relationship, or my *dad's* relationship? Decisions, decisions! Actually, Dad's old enough to sort out his own relationship, so mine won. I looked at the text message. *Cn U cm ovr now?*

Yes! Darien wanted me to go over to his place. Of course everyone knew where he lived because his dad runs the dry cleaner's in the High Street and Darien and his family live in the flat above it. Actually, though I'm not a snob or anything like that, I have to admit I was a tad shocked when I first found out. I mean, it's a bit of a come-down for his mum, an actress who used to work in the West End, living over a dry cleaner's – don't you think? Anyway, just then the front door slammed so I ran downstairs and grabbed my coat.

'Magenta! Come back here!' Dad shouted.

'Just want to catch Belinda,' I called as I went out of the door – not a total lie because I thought she might be up for giving me a lift and I might be able to smooth things over on the way into town.

Belinda had just got to her car when I caught up with her. 'Hi, Belinda, I wondered – if you're going home, you couldn't give me a lift up to the High Street, could you?'

She looked at me and gave a big sigh. 'I am not going to side with you against your father, Magenta.'

Honestly! Talk about a turncoat! 'Yes, but you said yourself Darien's nice and responsible.'

'And from what I've seen, he seems to be. I also think you and your dad need to talk this through –

this has got nothing to do with me.'

'Well, maybe not now but when you and Dad get married, you'll be my stepmum so it'll have everything to do with you then.'

She gave me this weird look. Then this really furious expression came across her face – even more furious than when she was telling me off at school that time. 'Married? Who said anything about us getting married?' Oops! 'Did your father tell you we were getting married?'

Eeeoo! 'No. Not at all.' Which was totally one hundred per cent true. Dad had never, ever, mentioned getting married.

She turned as though she was going to go back to the house but then seemed to change her mind. 'Magenta, I think you should go back home and think very carefully about what you want out of this relationship.' Only from the way she said it, it was almost like she was talking to herself, rather than me. Then she got into her car and drove off.

I looked back at our house and I could see Dad peering out from behind the curtains. No way was I going back to face that! After all, it was only seven o'clock. It wasn't like I was going to turn into a pumpkin any minute, so I legged it down the road as fast as I could and got to the bus stop just as a bus pulled up. Talk about fate shining on me.

I have to confess I felt a teensy bit nervous as I walked up the High Street. Well, that's a slight understatement: I was so nervous it felt as though my legs had turned into sticks of rubber and I thought I was going to be sick.

The dry cleaner's shop was locked up when I got there but there was a door next to it with an entry-phone on it. I pressed the buzzer and took a deep breath to try and calm myself.

'Yes?' this voice said.

'Erm, is Darien there please?'

'Who is that?' I couldn't make out if the voice was Darien's or not. It was definitely male and it didn't sound old enough to be his dad.

'It's me, Magenta.'

'Who?' Obviously, it couldn't have been Darien.

'Would you please tell Darien that Magenta's here?'

'This is Darien and who's . . . Hang on, do you mean Magenta from the play?'

'Yes, of course. You asked me to come over – remember?'

'What? Hold on, I'm coming down.' When he opened the door, I have to say, he didn't look quite as hunky in a crumpled old T-shirt as he did when he was at school. And, if I hadn't known better, I'd have thought he wasn't expecting me. I was beginning to feel a bit uneasy about the whole thing. It was a good job I'd actually spoken to him that afternoon, or I'd have thought that someone had been playing a trick on me. 'What do you want? What're you doing here?' He sounded a tad irritated and not at all pleased to see me.

I was completely gobsmacked! 'You sent me a text message asking me to come over.'

'I did *what*?' Honestly, he sounded really sneery and horrible. I was just about to get stroppy with him – I don't care if he *is* in Year 12 – when this woman came up and pushed past me.

'Scuse me.' She was wearing tatty old jogging bottoms, a nylon anorak and had a scarf round her head. I mean, excuse me for being a bit of a fashion snob but there's no way I'd be seen dressed like that outside a coalbunker.

'Hi, Mum!' Darien said to her. Mum? The famous actress? Surely not! And then I realised, she was probably still in costume. Wow, a famous actress had pushed past me.

Then Darien turned back to me. 'What are you talking about?'

Famous mother or no famous mother, I was feeling

a teensy bit peed off with his tone of voice. 'You asked me to come over.'

'Yeah! Like, in your dreams!' What a pig!

Luckily I hadn't deleted the message. 'OK then, look!' And I showed him – plus the previous one, where he'd asked me out. 'See!'

'Very nice but what gives you the idea that it's from me?'

'Durrr!' I was getting *extremely* peed off by this time. 'Your number!'

'Durrr! No, it isn't.'

'OK, so who was I talking to at half-past four today then, who answered this number and told me it was Darien?' There! Got him! I didn't know what his little game was but I was going to show him!

'Haven't a clue but I was having a driving lesson at half-past four this afternoon. Now if you've quite finished – push off!' And he shut the door in my face!

Can you believe it? What a rude and ignorant worm he was! And to think that Belinda had told Dad he was nice and responsible – huh! I don't think so! Well, the only thing left for me to do now was to phone the number again and find out who the dirty rotten lowlife was who'd set me up for this. I was so angry I nearly punched a hole in the phone as I pressed in the numbers.

'Magenta? Where are you? Your dad said you'd run off.'

I could not believe my ears. '*Daniel?* How could you? You . . . you . . .' And then an awful thought hit me. 'Where were you at half-past four today?'

'You know where I was. I was on the bus coming home from Magnus'. You rang me.' Uh-oh! I was getting a really bad feeling about this. 'Are you OK? Where are you?'

'I'm in the High Street.' I wasn't sure what was going on but I was beginning to think that emigration might be the only solution.

'Look, go to The Filling Station and I'll meet you there. Magnus was supposed to be coming over but I sent him a text about an hour ago and he hasn't turned up yet.'

Daniel was so sweet. It turns out that when he was with the Liable Twins, Angus had been messing around with his phone and must have sent that message to me as a joke. When I'd rung back to find out who it was, Daniel had been on the bus and hadn't quite heard me. He'd thought I'd said 'Daniel' not 'Darien'. Then tonight he'd sent Magnus a message to go over to his but had pressed 'MAG' and then 'OK', which sent it to me by mistake – and the rest, as Mr Jones-the-Bones know-it-all would say, is history. What a total and utter mess!

'I feel such an idiot!' I said as Daniel bought me another milk-shake. 'I hate stupid text messages.'

'I'll come round tomorrow and help you program in all your numbers. It just takes some getting used to, that's all.'

'And I hate that stupid Darien Quinn!'

Daniel smiled. 'What? You mean you're not turned on by his hermetically-sealed leather trousers?'

I started to giggle. 'I suppose he does look a bit of a prat, doesn't he?'

'A bit? He gives prats a bad name!'

Of course, once we got home, Dad blew a gasket and I was under house arrest for the entire weekend. Not that I minded; it's the dress rehearsal on Thursday and I've brought home some props that need finishing so I'll just stay in and do those.

'You know what they say – a bad dress rehearsal means a good performance?' Daniel had come round and was being really sweet. 'Tomorrow'll be fine. You'll see.'

'But it wasn't a bad dress rehearsal, was it? It wasn't a dress rehearsal at all!' I wailed. I knew he was doing his best to console me. And, I have to admit, he'd been a total star this afternoon. I don't know what I'd have done without him.

Things had been going really brilliantly this morning. For one thing, being involved in the props and scenery team for the play means that I got the whole of today off lessons. (The cast only get the afternoon off for the dress rehearsal, but the technical people, like me, have the whole day – how brilliant is that?) Not that it's a doss or anything: it's really hard work, putting the last-minute touches to stuff and making sure everything's in the right place for when it's needed. But, I have to tell you this, right: The best bit of the whole play for me is this mahoosive car that Belinda and I have built. It is *so* fantastic! We've made it out of cardboard over a wooden frame and it's suspended on ropes from these metal girders high above the stage. Then when it's not needed, we just put side scenery in front of it so that it's hidden from the audience. And we've done these different cardboard bodies for it as well, so that it looks tatty in one scene and all done up in another. It is so amazing. I feel really proud when I look at it. In fact, I was so excited about today that I even got in early this morning so that I could go through everything. And, actually, it's a good job too because when I checked the positioning of the car it was about a foot too far towards the front of the stage. The way they'd got it, all the scenery that came in front of it would have to be moved. I don't know who'd put it up but it was obviously someone who didn't know the play very well. Now I know that, technically, no one below Year 12 is supposed to go on the scaffold tower – but, there was no one around and it was going to be so much easier if I just popped up there and slid the ropes over a bit, rather than having to go off and find someone. So I did. I'll admit, it was a teensy bit scary up there but I don't really know what all the fuss is about. Health and safety or something. But anyway, it was no big deal. I thought I'd better not mention it to anyone though – just in case old Crusher got wind of it and sent in the heavy brigade or something.

Anyway, all the technical stuff this morning went brilliantly and, actually, I'll be really sad when Belinda leaves next week. She's being great at the moment. She explained that she'd been looking for another job for quite a while and that her dilemma had been about leaving me just before my GCSEs and not the other way round. But she's going to help me out at home – if my dad gets his act together, that is. Honestly! I don't know what's going on with him but he's growling about the house like a lion with toothache. No one can do a thing right and mentioning Belinda's name is on a par with signing your own death warrant. So I thought I'd sound out Belinda – subtly, of course.

'Have you spoken to Dad recently?' I said, casually. 'Just check that we've got everything for the sleepover scene ready, will you?' Not quite the response I'd hoped for – in fact, I thought Belinda sounded a tad irritated at the mention of Dad's name.

Things were looking a bit desperate on the wedding front. 'Have you seen him at all since last Friday?' I think I'd got just the right level of nonchalance.

'Magenta, can we stay focused on the play, please? What about the props for the milk bar scene?'

'Only he came home from Tai Chi early and . . .'

'Has that got anything at all to do with the task in hand, Magenta?' Oooooo! Tetch-ee! So I decided to let it drop for a while.

I went up to Daniel who was in the lighting box, looking terribly efficient. Actually, he's been very sweet all week since he came and rescued me from the High Street last Friday. I'm so glad we're friends again. You should've seen him during rehearsals walking around with his little head-set on saying things like, 'I'm on to it, mate,' and stuff like that. He looked so mature and responsible – it was really cute watching him. We've had rehearsals every day this week but so far I'd managed to avoid Darien – thank goodness! And I was hoping that it would stay that way, but no such luck. I was standing there in the lighting box (avoiding Ms Don't-talk-to-me-about-your-father) when Daniel beckoned me over.

'Look, I'm really sorry but there was a problem with Darien's radio mic earlier. We've fixed it now, so would you take it down to him in the dressing room?' Oh great! The last person in the world I wanted to have to talk to was Darien but I could see from the general panic in the box that they couldn't spare anyone else.

'Cheers, Daniel!'

'Sorry!'

Just what I needed! But never let it be said that I'm not mature enough to get over my disappointment. I'd show that skunk in leather cling-wrap that I was above his pretentious sneery insults. On the way down to the dressing room I was looking at his radio mic. All the main actors had them. They were these little boxy things that clipped on to the back of their costumes with a teensy microphone that pinned on to their lapel. It was amazing really that such a small thing could send sound all over the theatre. I was pressing this button and wondering what it did when suddenly Darien came out of the boys' toilets and started to go into the dressing room.

'Darien?'

'Not you again!' Honestly, I can't believe I never saw how rude he was before.

'The stage crew have sent this down. It's mended now.' I handed him the mic and, would you believe it, he didn't even say thank you! What an arrogant pig!

It was almost time to begin and people were wandering into the hall from the dressing rooms so I went over to the back stage area. I was thinking how blind I'd been over Darien and that Daniel had been so right when he'd said it would be an insult to prats to include Darien. Then suddenly, booming out of the speakers in the theatre I could hear Darien's voice.

'. . . only went and turned up on my doorstep . . . Can you believe it? I've got my very own stalker . . . Yeah, that little kid with the braces who mooches around like an motorway pile-up waiting to happen . . . I swear on my mother's reputation, dahling, there she was like some love-struck Metal Mickey standing on my doorstep . . .' I felt sick! This wasn't happening – surely? '. . . Actually, I'm amazed she's allowed in a theatre with all that metal in her mouth. You'd think it would interfere with the sound equipment, wouldn't you? And – get the irony – her name's Magenta. An anagram of *a magnet* – get it? Attracts metal?'

Then Samantha Campion, Daniel's ex-older woman, came charging by screaming into her head set, 'What the hell's going on up there? Faders down! Take the faders down!' Then she patted me on the shoulder as she went past. 'Don't worry about him, Magenta, everyone knows what he's like.'

Easy for her to say! She wasn't the one who'd just been slagged off and humiliated. I wanted a dirty great hole to open up in the middle of the stage and swallow me. This was too awful for words. It was like my brain had gone into meltdown. I couldn't think what to do. I just stood there, frozen, like a rabbit in the headlights.

Belinda put her arm round me. 'I'm going to go and speak to Darien and tell him that I think a full and public apology is in order.'

Like that would reverse time! What use was an apology? He'd already said all that stuff to the entire world. I had to get out of there. I had to go home. I had to leave school – the country – the universe! People were staring at me. Never in my entire life has the phrase 'Beam me up Scotty' had more urgency. Arlette and Seema were mouthing stuff that I'm sure was supposed to be reassuring but everything was looking blurred. I felt my bottom lip begin to tremble. Oh joy! Just to crown everything, I was going to cry in public. Brilliant!

And then another voice came out of the speakers. It was familiar but I wasn't really taking it in. 'Erm, this is an important announcement.' It was Daniel's voice and I could see him now, standing next to Arlette and speaking into her radio mic. 'The thing about radio mics is – you turn them off when you're not actually on stage.' He was looking up at the sound and lighting box and waving his hand upwards. I didn't know what he was doing but his voice suddenly seemed really loud, like it was echoing from every corner. 'So when someone who pretends that his mother is a famous actress does something as stupid as leaving his mic on . . .' everyone turned and looked in Darien's direction, '. . . you might begin to wonder whether or not the theatre really is in his blood. And the truth is . . .' You could've dropped a pin in there – honestly, I didn't know what Daniel was playing at but he certainly had everyone's attention – '. . . Darien's – or should I say, Darren's . . .'

'Why, you, little . . .' I thought Darien was going to plant one on Daniel.

'Your real name *is* Darren, isn't it?' If it hadn't been for Hayden and Ben restraining Darien (or Darren, or whoever he was), I think Daniel might have had another black eye. 'So, what I wanted to say was that Darren's mother *did* used to work at the London Palladium but . . .'

'I'm warning you!' Darren/Darien screamed.

'But she didn't so much tread the boards as sweep them. She was the cleaner there. Isn't that true, *Darren*?' There was a gasp from everyone in the hall. 'And the other thing I want to say is, it isn't metal braces that give a person an ugly mouth, it's the things that they say!'

There was a huge cheer from everyone and then people started clapping Daniel. And then the most amazing thing happened, people started looking at me and clapping me too. Wow! I mean, how amazing was that? I started to go all teary and when I looked at Daniel he was smiling at me in such a sweet way that I went all warm and fuzzy inside. But then Darren/Darien pushed Hayden and Ben away and stormed out. Mr Marlowe went after him but, apparently, he said he wasn't coming back. Drama queen in the extreme!

After that, it all got a bit panicky. Mr Grimsby and Mr Marlowe sat down for a few minutes and then swapped everyone's parts around – just like that! Talk about last minute – but everyone more or less knows everyone else's lines anyway. Hayden's now playing Danny, which means that he and Seema get to snog at the end, which will be so cool. And Ben's been moved from the chorus and he and Arlette get to be all smoochy too. How excellent is that? So this afternoon was just a run-through and we're having the dress rehearsal tomorrow morning before the first performance for the school in the afternoon and the final show for the parents and governors tomorrow night.

But, satisfying as it was to hear Daniel dish the dirt on mongrel-features, it didn't take away all the stuff Darien had said about me, so I was still feeling a bit low when Daniel came round in the evening.

'I thought you were brilliant the way you handled all the stuff that scum-bag was saying about you,' he said. 'A lot of people would've got really upset.'

'D'you think?' Actually, I thought Daniel was a total hero. And he'd looked so hunky in his head-set this afternoon. I decided to take back everything I'd said about him since we broke up. He's one pretty amazing guy. I patted the bed for him to come and sit down next to me. 'You didn't have to say all that stuff, you know – about braces not being ugly and everything.'

He sat down and took hold of my hand. 'I meant every word of it, Magenta.' Wow! He suddenly looked so gorgeous. I couldn't believe we'd ever finished.

'Daniel?' I could feel myself moving closer and closer to him. I realised my eyes had homed in on his lips. And, oooh, did he have the most gorgeous lips!

'Yeah?' His voice sounded so husky!

'D'you think we might . . .'

Oh great! His mobile phone started ringing! 'Hi Justine.' Gggrrr! My wretched cousin has to poke her nose in everywhere! 'That sounds a brilliant idea . . . Yes . . . I'll think about it . . . Cheers, Juss . . . Speak to you later.' He turned back to me. 'What were you saying?'

'Forget it!' Did I really say I couldn't believe we'd ever finished? Talk about short-term memory loss! What was I thinking of? No way was I going to get conned by that smooth-talking, two-timing slimeball again. 'Thanks for coming round, Daniel. I'll see you tomorrow. Bye.' I practically had to push him out of the French windows. Talk about a narrow escape!

And I've decided – I am never, ever, **ever**,

ever, going to have anything to do with boys again.
EVER!

11
Daniel

'Hello! Earth to Dan!' Samantha was waving this white plastic bottle in front of my face. 'Wake up, Sunshine – it's like you've been on a different planet all morning.'

Yes – the planet of hopelessness! Every time I seem to be making progress with Magenta, it's like – WHAM! Straight between the eyes with the Sledgehammer of Doom! Last night I'd have taken bets on the fact that she was going to kiss me. You should have seen her – she was so lovely and she was saying things like how grateful she was and what a hero I'd been and then she came right up close. I mean, really close – so that our lips were like, this far apart. (You need to use your imagination here and picture my thumb and finger about a millimetre apart.) And, I swear to you, she was the one doing all the up close and personal stuff. But then my phone only went and rang – talk about bad timing – and suddenly, it was like I'd become radioactive. She couldn't get me out of her room fast enough.

I know it's all to do with this stupid feud with her cousin but she won't even talk about it. Ever since Curtis' party, every time I try to explain about Justine, she shuts her eyes, sticks her fingers in her ears and starts shouting, 'La la la la la la. Not listening! La la la!' (Actually, she looks really cute when she does that.) But it's hardly going to lead to a communication breakthrough, is it?

'You're not blaming yourself for Darien bottling out, are you?' Samantha asked.

'What? Oh, no.'

'Good! Because, apart from old Grimbum, I think everyone else will be glad to see the back of him. Anyway, take this bottle of smoke fluid down to the props team, will you, and get someone to put it in the smoke machine? Then come back and we'll run through the sound effects again.'

I should've been ecstatic; this was going to be my big moment. Kiran, who had been in charge of sound effects, had just had a message that his granddad had been taken ill, so he'd gone home and Samantha had promoted me to take over. My big break and all I could think of was my big break-up. I didn't know how I was ever going to get back with Magenta.

I'd been trying to get some male perspective on my predicament at registration before I had to go off to the rehearsal. Not that the guys were being much help. 'Come on, you know Magenta's the only girl I've ever really fancied. It was only ever going to be a one night thing with me and Juss. But how do I get that through to Magenta when she keeps doing this la la la thing?'

'Just chill, mate. It'll happen.' I wanted to believe Magnus but I was getting sick of waiting. I wanted some sort of guarantee.

'Or you could try kidnapping her, tying her hands behind her back so she can't stick her fingers in her ears, and then telling her.' Why do Spud's ideas always have that ring of insanity to them? 'Or' – I couldn't wait for part two – '*I* could kidnap her for you.' Nice try, Spud!

'I'm telling you, don't rush it,' Magnus said.

'Anyway, if Justine was only a one nighter, why is she still ringing you a month down the road? Eh?' Spud tapped the side of his nose like some second-rate private eye who pretends he knows something.

'Because we're friends.'

'Yeah! Right!' I thought mates were supposed to be supportive but I'm beginning to think that Spud's dictionary has a different definition.

'Anyway, she's got a new boyfriend now. And she says it helps her to talk to me so she can understand about boys and stuff like that.'

'OooOoooo! Obi-*Dan* Kenobi! Relationship guru and Jedi knight in shining armour.' Spud was doing his imitation of a light sabre round my head – but he sounded more like a bluebottle having an asthma attack.

'Leave it out!' I was getting really pissed off with him. 'Anyway, Justine's not the issue here. It's the Magenta situation that's doing my head in.'

'Ain't never gonna happen, mate!' Angus, the Twisted Fire-Starter, was rubbing a piece of dowel between his hands and trying to create a small inferno on the desk like the Native Americans used to. Everyone knew that even someone as dedicated to incineration as Angus would never manage to ignite it because the desk was made of formica. We didn't tell him that though because at least it kept him occupied.

'Just play it cool,' Magnus said. 'She'll come round. Everyone can see she's hot for you.' Now Magnus is what I call a true friend.

'Really?'

'Nah! He's just saying that to make you feel better,' Spud chipped in. 'Personally, I don't think she's over me yet. Here, Angus, try it on this ruler. Wood on wood's much more likely to work.' Which just goes to prove that half a brain cell really is far more dangerous than no brain cell at all.

I was in danger of losing the will to live, so I decided that it was time to go to my rehearsal. 'Later!' I said.

'Hey, Danno! Chill! Let the force be with you!' Magnus called out.

'Yeah! Treat her keen and keep her mean!' Spud added. I'm starting to think that, with the exception of Magnus, my social circle is rapidly descending from *really average* to *seriously defective*. But I'll sort that out later; for the moment my love life (or lack of it) has got to take precedence.

So we'd got through the dress rehearsal and, actually, it had gone worryingly well; no major blips or anything. When you consider that I'd been on autopilot, Magenta had been skulking in the wings like Sulky McSulky and half the cast had taken on different parts less than twenty-four hours ago, such a flawless dress rehearsal had seriously freaky implications. Mind you, Mr Marlowe *had* been sitting on the front row like the King of Karaoke with a flip-chart that had everyone's lines on. He must've been up all night doing that.

Everyone (except me – and probably Magenta) was on a bit of a high because it had gone so well. We were setting up for the afternoon performance to the school but, even though my body was in the lighting box, my mind was backstage, tying itself in knots over Magenta. So, when Samantha handed me the plastic bottle of smoke fluid, she might as well have handed me the key to my future happiness. It was just the chance I'd been looking for. There hadn't been any time to talk to Magenta this morning – I'd caught glimpses of her every now and then but we'd all been really busy; this was my golden opportunity. I ran down backstage and there she was, manoeuvring the picnic bench into place for the first scene. She was wearing an old T-shirt and jeans and she had a bandanna on her head. She looked so beautiful – in a casual sort of way.

'Hi,' I said, hoping she might be a bit more friendly than she had been last night. 'Apparently you need some more smoke fluid.' I tried to remember how I'd smiled at her just before she said what a hero I'd been, so that the moment might be rekindled – but I think I must've got it wrong.

'OK, thanks,' she said, in a way that was about as friendly as your average razor wire.

Maybe Magnus was right; I should just be cool and wait for her to come round. I cleared my throat and tried the businesslike approach. 'Do you know what to do with it?'

'Erm, no but I'm sure someone will. Thank you. Bye.'

Obviously businesslike wasn't working either. 'Look, Magenta, are you upset about Justine?'

'La la la la la! Don't want to talk about it. Just put the stuff down there and I'll sort it out.' Did I say she looked cute when she did that? Well, today she looked about as cute as a great white shark with PMS. I was starting to get really annoyed with her.

Magnus' theory hadn't worked and I was getting desperate. When in desperation, follow Spud's advice. I pulled her fingers out of her ears. 'How? How will you sort it out? How will you sort anything out when you avoid stuff all the time?'

'Don't start getting all macho with me, Daniel Davis.' She grabbed the bottle out of my hand and began looking all over it as though she was trying to find some instructions.

'Give it to me. I'll do it.' I took the bottle back and unscrewed the cap ready to put on the other feeder cap – the one with a tube coming out of it for pouring the fluid out of the bottle and into the machine. But before I could screw on the feeder cap, Magenta snatched it back.

'I can manage, thank you!' Only she obviously couldn't because as she grabbed the open bottle, smoke fluid splashed out and a huge wave slopped on to the floor. 'Now look what you've done!' she snapped at me.

'What's going on?' Ms Lovell came up.

'Daniel's spilt smoke fluid everywhere.' Can you believe that? I was furious! I was rapidly sinking to the Angus line of thought that, actually, this was never going to happen. And, actually, if Magenta was going to be this unreasonable, maybe I didn't *want* anything to happen anyway!

'It doesn't matter who spilt it, it needs mopping up. Magenta, sort that out please and find out whose lunchbox this is for the first scene. It shouldn't have been left here.' She handed Magenta a lunchbox.

Magenta completely ignored me. 'Oh, Nadine!' she called out. 'Is this yours?'

Just then, Samantha's voice came through my head set asking me to go back up to the box and I could hear people starting to file into the hall. I was still really annoyed with Magenta but this performance was what we'd been working towards for about two months. I wasn't going to blow it. I took a couple of deep breaths, you know, like boxers do before a fight. 'I need to go now. I'll catch you later.' I said.

'Whatever!'

As I turned to go back upstairs Nadine came across to collect her lunchbox.

'Hi, Daniel! I thought you were brilliant yesterday, you know – the way you stood up to that slime ball.'

'Thanks, Nadine.' I hoped Magenta had heard that and I think she must have because she pushed the lunchbox into Nadine's hands very roughly.

'Cheers, Magenta. I've been looking everywhere for that. Must go! Good luck both of you!' Nadine started to go back towards the dressing room but then 'Aaaaaggggh!'

One minute she'd been walking upright, the next, she was skidding across the puddle of smoke fluid at an angle of forty-five degrees with her mouth opening and closing like a goldfish on water skis. Then suddenly, all I could see was a pair of white tennis shoes and acres of frothy netting as her legs shot up in the air. Magenta and I ran over to her but she was buried underneath her ra-ra petticoat so that we had to trace the sound of her moans to find out if she was OK.

Magenta was flapping about like a chicken on the verge of decapitation. 'Oh, this is terrible! Nadine! Nadine!' Then she turned to me. 'Do something, Daniel!'

Now, if Nadine had required a soft lighting effect,

or a piece of cable running round her, then I think I can modestly say that I would've been the man to help. My first aid skills, however, don't really stretch much beyond the sticking plaster level.

'Like what?'

And Samantha, who is the queen of cool normally and, even if the four-minute warning went, would probably still find time to run a sound check, was starting to reach a crescendo in my ear. 'Ten minutes to curtain-up and we need to run through these sound effects, Dan. Get your bum up here pronto!'

'I'll be there as soon as I can, Samantha – we've got a slight crisis down here.'

'Slight?' Magenta said. 'If we lose any more of the cast we might as well do it with cardboard cut-outs!'

I could hear Mr Gimsby's voice booming down the corridor. 'Places, everyone!'

'You have got to get him away from here, Daniel. He'll only blame me. He blames me for everything. Go and get Belinda!'

'Oh, my back!' Nadine moaned. At least she was conscious. 'Oh, my foot! Oh, my arm.'

Ms Lovell was brilliant. I'm still not sure how she did it but Mr Grimsby didn't find out about the switch until the curtains opened and then it was too

215

late for him to do anything about it. Mrs Delaney took Nadine off to Casualty in her car, while Magenta put on Nadine's costume and covered for her as Joan – which, when you think about it, makes sense because she'd covered for her in rehearsals so she sort of knew the part – ish. And then she was really sweet to me.

'Thanks, Daniel. I'm sorry I was a bit off this morning.'

'No worries. And, goo—' I'd been going to say good luck but that's supposed to be bad luck in the theatre. If you want to wish actors good luck you're supposed to say break a leg. But I thought, in the circumstances, that might be tempting fate a bit. 'Go for it,' I said. I was so relieved that we seemed to be back on track again.

Anyway, she was brilliant. Oh, you should've seen her: I felt so proud as I looked down from the lighting box. It didn't matter that she'd been crabby with me – she'd obviously been under a lot of stress. But when I saw her on stage, she looked amazing. And she was doing pretty well with the words too, thanks to Mr Marlowe's prompt board. We were up to the sleepover scene and all the girls were at one side of the stage and then there was a partition to the other side of the stage which was meant to be the street outside. We'd just got to the part where Sandy goes outside to sing her solo. Samantha tapped me on the shoulder. Because of all the Nadine stuff we hadn't had chance to run through the sound effects properly so she was reminding me every time. But, to be honest, it was starting to get on my nerves a bit. It was like she didn't trust me and I don't know why she'd been getting paranoid in the first place; Kiran had been so efficient, even a total moron could've taken over.

'You ready?' she mouthed.

I nodded. I checked my script. We were coming up for the sound effect of an owl hooting as Sandy wanders out on to the balcony. 'Gold animal noises CD. Track 78.' Kiran had written next to the cue. I took the CD out of the rack and lined up track seventy-eight. My eyes were on the stage. I had one eye on Seema so that I knew when to play the owl hoot but the other eye was on Magenta. I knew I wouldn't be able to speak to her during the interval now that she was in the cast but I was determined to catch her inbetween performances. I couldn't wait to tell her how proud I was of her.

I moved my attention to Seema as she walked through the partition and began looking wistfully around. There was a hush over the audience.

'Now!' Samantha whispered. I pressed play and moved the faders up. Eeek! Instead of a plaintive owl hooting, the noise of stampeding elephants trumpeted around the hall. The whole school erupted with jeers and catcalls. What a nightmare!

'What's happened?' I looked to Samantha. 'This is track seventy-eight.'

I looked down at the audience and felt sick. People were banging their feet and making mock elephant noises. Teachers were walking up and down the aisles trying to keep everyone quiet. It was chaos.

Samantha leapt across the box and ejected the CD. 'Dan! That's the silver animal noises CD. Kiran's list says gold.' She swapped them over and the owl hooted as it should've done.

'Sorry,' I whispered. 'I couldn't see in this light.' My big chance and I'd blown it – and in front of the whole school. All my mates had witnessed it. Worse still, my brother Joe would never let me live this down. But even worse still, it'd happened in front of Magenta – just as things were sorting themselves out again. What a muppet I was! I couldn't look at the stage, in case she was laughing at me. All credit to Seema, though – she kept her cool through the whole thing and, actually, when I *was* brave enough to look at Magenta, she did seem to be looking quite sympathetic.

Things were going fairly well until almost at the end. It was the car race scene and I'd been right on cue with my engine revving sound effect but it seems that whoever had taken over from Magenta on the smoke machine was a tad over-enthusiastic. There was so much smoke that it was difficult to see across the stage. I know California has a smog problem but this was a bit like trying to watch the play through porridge. Then, all of a sudden a klaxon sounded. No one took any notice at first – I think everyone thought it was another sound effect cock-up but then the Crusher started to shout, 'Lights up please! Can we have the lights up?' People were filing out and teachers were directing every one out of the hall. I did a quick recce round the hall just to check that Angus hadn't been up to his tricks behind the seats but he was filing out with the rest of them, so I was pretty sure it was just a false alarm.

'What do we do?' I asked Samantha.

She shrugged. 'Better get out, I suppose.'

'But it's only the smoke machine that's overdosed. It's not as though we're going to get burnt to a crisp or anything.'

'Come along you lot, outside on to the playing

field.' Mr Grimsby was standing in the doorway fuming. To be honest, it wouldn't have surprised me if it was the smoke coming out of his ears that had set off the fire alarm.

Of course, by the time the hall had cleared of smoke and people could get back inside, it was almost half-past three and people had started to drift off home. So the rest of the production was abandoned. Everyone was gutted. All that excitement and preparation! The atmosphere was terrible. We'd got one final performance in the evening for the parents and governors and, to be fair the Crusher had said that anyone who wanted to could come back this evening to see the rest of the play for free. But generally speaking the cast and stage crew were pretty flat. I had hoped that Magenta and I could have our chat, but no one felt like talking much. We just sat around eating our sandwiches and then got on with setting up again. Talk about a damp squib.

The nice thing about being up in the lighting box is that you can see who's coming into the hall and it was nice to see the posse coming in for a second dose; Spud, Magnus and Angus all gave a thumbs up to the box. Maybe I won't change my circle of friends after all. I noticed a wheelchair being brought down the aisle to the front and when I looked more closely, Nadine was sitting in it. She had her arm in a sling and her leg was all bandaged up but at least she hadn't been kept in hospital. And then Mum came in with Curtis and Florence and they sat right at the back, underneath the box. Unfortunately, a reluctant Joe was bringing up the rear of the group. He looked up, put his shoulder to his nose (like we used to when we were little and played at being elephants), and started flapping his arm up and down like an elephant's trunk. Great! Just what I needed, a heckler in the crowd. But actually it didn't matter because Kiran's granddad had suddenly perked up a bit, so Kiran had come back to do the sound effects for the final performance.

'You did a great job, Dan – really,' Samantha said. 'Everyone makes mistakes. That's how we learn.' That's what Mum says too but, have you noticed that when you're making the mistakes, it somehow doesn't seem like you're learning anything? It just seems like you're making a complete prat of yourself! 'Anyway, if you'd go on follow spot this evening, that would be great.' A follow spot is this dirty great spotlight that's on a tripod on the balcony above the hall. You have to stand with your arms stretched out, one on the front and one at the back to hold it still so that it doesn't wobble while it's trained on the stage. Then you have to follow the actors around with it so that they stay in the spotlight.

'That's cool,' I said. I didn't mind doing follow spot but it doesn't half make your arms ache. Of course, the one consolation was that at least I couldn't cause herds of marauding elephants to make their way on to a quiet suburban street scene.

As we got the five-minute call I started to get all tingly again. Mr Marlowe had given everyone a little pep talk and it seemed to have done the trick.

'Just think of the afternoon's performance as the dress rehearsal. And, I think you'll all agree, it was fairly disastrous.' Everyone gave a sort of murmur of agreement. 'Well then, that must mean that tonight is going to be a success! Let's really pull all the stops out. Forget this afternoon. Kiran's back on sound effects.' There was a small cheer and then people looked at me in a distinctly pitying way. Great! 'And the smoke machine's been sorted. It seems that the settings had been turned up by mistake.' I'm sure I saw Magenta bite her bottom lip when he said that, but it doesn't matter any more. She's an actor now and a brilliant one – in the circumstances. 'So just let this afternoon go. We've got the Mayor coming tonight and a full contingent of governors. Let's show

them what we're made of. Let's go, go, go, go, GO!'
We were all in a big circle and I looked across and
caught Magenta's eye. She looked so excited. I smiled
at her but Seema and Arlette pulled her away into
the wings so we didn't get the chance to speak.

Anyway, the whole atmosphere changed after that.
There was a real buzz about the place. I took up my
position on the balcony. My light was all set up; my
headset was in place – not that it was much use. Noel,
the other boy on follow spot, has a sinus problem so
the only thing anyone can hear when they try to listen
to the lighting people is Darth Vader-type heavy
breathing.

Suddenly the orchestra started playing the
overture and the curtains went back. Wow! It felt like
I'd swallowed a tonne of fizzing candy. There was
Magenta in the background and she looked boom!
Nadine's pink cardigan really suited her – she's so
beautiful! There were a few times during the play
when I saw her reading her lines from Mr Marlowe's
flip chart but so were other people. I just hoped old
Grimbum realised what he'd missed, not giving her
a part in the first place. Although, to be fair, she's
been brilliant with the sets too.

We were coming up to the climax of the play;
the race scene and the whole performance had

been brilliant. Kiran hadn't made a single cock-up with the sound effects, no one had made any major bloomers with their lines and there'd been no accidents. The whole place was electric. I can see how people get hooked on the theatre. Hayden West, who had taken over as Danny, and a sixth-former who was playing one of his rivals, had cardboard cars strapped on to them. Noel and I had to follow them round the stage and hall with our lights as they had their car race. I really had to pay attention for this scene and make sure my light stayed on Hayden. Seema was sitting on her own at one side of the stage with a fixed spotlight on her and the rest of the cast were watching the race. Magenta was standing on the back of the main car with her hand above her eyes. She looked so dramatic – a bit like Kate Winslet looking over the bow of the *Titanic*.

But as I was watching Magenta and waiting for the cue for the start of the race I noticed a weird thing. It looked as though the big model car had been moved back a couple of feet. I couldn't understand it. When we'd been setting up earlier in the week Samantha noticed that the props team had tied the ropes of the car to girders that meant the ropes hung right in front of one of the fixed spotlights. So some of the sixth-formers had had to go up the scaffold tower and move the whole thing forward a bit so that the ropes weren't touching the lights. With the amount of heat those lights give out, it could've set fire to the rope – although don't tell Angus. Now, though, it looked as though someone had moved it back. Being up on the balcony I had a pretty clear view of the roof area and – eeeek! Oh no! One of the ropes supporting the car had started smouldering! And, worse still, Magenta was standing on the car. If the rope burned through, the car would fall down and she was going to be terribly injured.

'Bang!' The starting pistol went off, which was the cue for the car race to begin. I was desperate. It was crucial that my spotlight was on Hayden West but if I didn't put out the fire there'd be carnage stage left!

'Help, somebody!' I whispered into the mouthpiece of my headset. No answer – Noel really should get his sinuses seen to! I looked around for someone to tell, but there was no one else on the balcony. 'Can anybody hear me?' I said again. This was awful. I was trying to keep my light on Hayden but also trying to keep an eye on the rope as well. Why wasn't the klaxon sounding? It'd gone off this afternoon for an over-zealous smoke machine but when the real thing was out there threatening to burn down the entire theatre – zilch! I looked at the stage. The actors were jumping up and down cheering the car racers and Magenta was jumping up and down too – on the back of the model that was soon going to plummet to the ground! It was no good. I let go of the light and ran.

There was a universal, 'Uh!' from the audience as my light swung down to face the floor of the balcony and Hayden West was plunged into darkness in his bid to beat the sixth-former round the back of the hall but I didn't care. Magenta's life was more important than a car race, or a school play. And I didn't even care if I lost my place in the stage crew. I leapt down the stairs three at a time. Down the corridor outside the hall and into the side door that led into the wings. I looked up and the flames were enormous by now. I saw the car jolt slightly as the rope burned through.

'Magentaaaaaaaaaaa!' I ran across the stage and flying tackled her. (Dad said I wouldn't regret being dragged along to rugby club when I was ten but I didn't believe him at the time.) I grabbed her round the knees, knocking her off the car and we landed on the stage.

'Daniel! What the . . .?' she screamed.

There was a gasp from the audience and cast. Then one or two voices started to shout, 'Fire!' And just at that moment there was a humungous *ping* from the ceiling as the rope finally snapped. I looked up at Magenta – phew! She was safe. But then I saw this look of terror on her face.

'Daniel!'

Eeeee-ow! The huge model car came crashing down – right on top of me!

P.S.

Oh! My! God! You would not believe how exciting things have turned out. First of all, Daniel only went and saved my life – in front of all the parents and teachers and governors and everybody! I mean – how romantic is that? Didn't I tell you what a hero he was? Honestly, he really is such a star.

Of course there was a teensy bit of a downside because although he stopped me getting crushed to death, he ended up with a broken leg himself. But, on the positive side – he has crutches! I mean that is so manly and *Treasure Island*-ish, don't you think? And, if I'm being honest, I've always secretly hankered after crutches – ever since Joe fell out of a tree when he was seven. Oh, I was so jealous – Joe's crutches and Sarah Scrimshaw's elastoplast eye-patch – both to die for!

Anyway, it was all really dramatic because Daniel was trapped under this huge model, which didn't fall apart when it hit the ground, I'm proud to say. (Testament to our good workmanship, I think!) Then this piece of flaming rope fell on top of it and the cardboard side piece caught fire. People were running everywhere and Angus Lyle was jumping up and down like a jack-in-the-box on a bouncy castle screaming, 'Oh yes! Genius!' Teachers and sixth-formers were trying to take control but no one was listening. On a scale of 'laid-back' to 'total mayhem', the whole place was completely off the scale. According to Belinda, it turns out that the Grim Reaper had only gone and turned off the fire alarm after the whole smoke machine fiasco, so he's now up on a disciplinary hearing. (Yes! It's so nice to know that there is justice in the world.) And the Chief Fire Officer wants the school's fire-drill policy overhauled and an inquiry into how it happened. Uh-oh! I've just had a terrible thought – I hope it wasn't anything to do with when I moved the ropes yesterday morning? Nah! Couldn't possibly be!

And, guess what, Daniel's only going to be recommended for a bravery award. Plus, he's going to be made Stage Crew Health and Safety rep next year. How fantastic is that – a boyfriend with an award *and* a title!

But the best thing was, while the Crusher and the Mayor were getting people out through the fire escapes, Dad saw that Belinda and I were trying to lift the car off Daniel's leg. He came charging down the aisle, leapt on to the stage like Arnold Schwarzenegger (OK – so I'm using poetic licence but humour me) and lifted the burning frame up so that we could pull Daniel free. Wow! I mean, correct me if I'm wrong but do I have the most amazing father in the world as well as the most amazing boyfriend, or what?

And then, when I was waiting for the ambulance with Daniel, things got even better! I could see Dad and Belinda being really intense and I was thinking, uh-oh, back to the drawing board on the whole stepmother thing when, suddenly, Dad put his arms round Belinda and they snogged! I mean, I don't want to get too graphic here but I'm pretty sure tongues were involved. And in public too! (I still can't decide whether it was cool or embarrassingly gross.) But when they came over to where we were, they both looked so happy. I felt all gooey inside, so I reckon it was pretty cool.

'Magenta,' Dad said, 'we want you to be the first to know. Belinda's asked me to marry her.' I bet if I hadn't put the idea into her head, she'd never have thought of it. Didn't I tell you I'd help things along? Wow, I am so good at this matchmaking thing.

'And your dad's said yes,' Belinda added. Then they gave each other this big cuddle. Oh, it was so sweet. I haven't seen Dad that happy for years. And then I had a brainwave. I thought, if Belinda can do it, so can I. I turned to Daniel. 'Daniel, I'm really sorry I got the wrong end of the stick. Will you go out with me again?' And he said yes! I'm so glad we're back together again. I put my arms round him, but it was before his leg had been set and he was still moaning quite a bit, so he suggested we save the celebration for later.

Anyway, I've said I'll go round to Daniel's tonight to do some really cool artwork on his plaster. And I'm already thinking about what I can wear for the wedding. I can't wait. Wow! I am so going to design my own bridesmaid outfit! How brilliant will that be?

A note from the author

People have asked me if Magenta is based on a real person and, I'm relieved to say, the answer is NO! However, if I'm being honest, I was a bit of a disaster-zone when I was thirteen, although nothing compared to Madge. I must give credit where it's due though - the idea for Magenta's pottery antics came from my brother, who really did try to throw a pot using an electric drill - don't try it at home!

MAGENTA ORANGE

Echo Freer

Magenta Orange has the world at her feet. If she could just stop tripping over them.

Bright, sassy and massively accident prone, Magenta's seen as a jinx by her mates – and a disaster zone by the boy of her dreams. Blind to the longing looks of her best friend, Daniel, and the sweet nothings of school freak, Spud, she's set her sights on year 11 hottie, Adam Jordan – and she'll risk everything, even total humiliation, in her relentless pursuit of a date . . .

'A wicked, witty read – 5/5!' *Mizz* magazine